To: **Meredith West**
From: **Lucy West**
Subject: **You think *you* need help?!**

Why did you make me fly back to England
with Guy Dangerfield? You *know* how much
I dislike that smooth, charming kind of
Englishman! I don't care how helpful he
is, or how nice he was to take me out for
dinner and let me stay at his (incredibly
posh!) flat. Really, I don't.

He bet me that I couldn't stick at a job,
so I went out and got one—in his office!
Now we'll see who has a problem with
commitment....

Lucy xxx

Bridegroom Boss

Hal Granger runs a busy cattle station.
He can't afford the time to be distracted.

Guy Dangerfield is a successful, charming
businessman. He's far too busy playing the field
to commit to one girl.

Until two sisters shake up their lives!

In September

Outback Boss, City Bride
Join Meredith as she finds herself
stranded in the Outback. The only compensation
is her *very* attractive boss!

This month

Appointment at the Altar
Single in the city, Lucy's looking for a new job
and a new life. She doesn't intend to add new love
to her list, until she meets utterly irresistible tycoon
Guy Dangerfield!

JESSICA HART
Appointment at the Altar

Bridegroom Boss

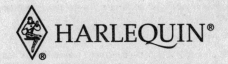

HARLEQUIN®

TORONTO • NEW YORK • LONDON
AMSTERDAM • PARIS • SYDNEY • HAMBURG
STOCKHOLM • ATHENS • TOKYO • MILAN • MADRID
PRAGUE • WARSAW • BUDAPEST • AUCKLAND

ISBN-13: 978-0-373-03987-6
ISBN-10:   0-373-03987-5

APPOINTMENT AT THE ALTAR

First North American Publication 2007.

Copyright © 2007 by Jessica Hart.

www.eHarlequin.com

Printed in U.S.A.

Jessica Hart was born in West Africa, and has suffered from itchy feet ever since. She has traveled and worked around the world in a wide variety of interesting but very lowly jobs, all of which have provided inspiration to draw from when it comes to the settings and plots of her stories. Now she lives a rather more settled existence in York, England, where she has been able to pursue her interest in history—although she still yearns sometimes for wider horizons. If you'd like to know more about Jessica, visit her Web site, www.jessicahart.co.uk.

For Stella and Julia, my City Screen plotting team

CHAPTER ONE

LUCY leant on the fence and watched Kevin, perched on a rail on the far side of the corral, waiting his turn at bareback bronc riding. In his Akubra hat, checked shirt and dusty boots, he was outback man incarnate. Strong, silent, lean-jawed, quiet-eyed…he made all her other boyfriends look like silly boys.

Not that he was a boyfriend, exactly, much as she would want to have been able to say so. But she was madly in love with him, and he *had* kissed her the other night. Things could only get better.

She sighed happily. In London now it would be cold and grey, but here she was in the red heart of Australia with its bright, brassy light and its fierce heat. Closing her eyes with a blissful shiver, Lucy turned her face up to the sunlight and breathed in the smell of dust and horses. She could hear the *'hup! hup!'* cries of the men coaxing reluctant animals into the chute and feel the sun beating on to her borrowed hat.

I'm happy, she thought.

'Well, if it isn't Cinderella!'

The amused voice in her ear froze her smile and her eyes snapped open. She didn't need to turn her head to know who was standing beside her. There was only one person out here with that accent.

That *English* accent, reeking of privilege and the most expensive education British money could buy.

Guy Dangerfield.

She had been delighted that morning to find herself squeezed into a truck with Kevin and the other stockmen when they left Wirrindago. There had been no sign of either her intimidating boss, Hal Granger, or his deeply annoying English cousin, which meant that they could all relax and have a good time at the rodeo. But now here was Guy, after all, looking irritatingly handsome and sophisticated and utterly out of place in the outback.

'Oh,' she said, not bothering to disguise her lack of enthusiasm. 'It's you.'

'It is,' Guy agreed.

Lucy hated the way he could say something perfectly unexceptional like that with a straight face and yet still make it sound as if he were laughing at her. It was something to do with the ripple of amusement in his voice, or maybe it was to do with his blue, blue eyes, currently hidden by ridiculously mirrored sunglasses, where a smile always seemed to be lurking even if he was only asking her to pass the toast.

What's so funny? she wanted to yell at him, but she had the nasty feeling that the answer would be her. Nobody else at Wirrindago seemed to find him annoying. They all thought he was great.

Lucy couldn't understand it. Guy had the kind of assurance that she always associated with generations of privilege and a gold-plated trust fund, and she didn't trust his practised charm for a moment. The self-deprecating humour and oh-so-engaging smile were completely wasted on her.

'Why do you always call me Cinderella?' she asked irritably.

'Because you're very pretty and you never seem to be allowed out of the kitchen,' said Guy.

'I'm a cook,' she reminded him with a touch of sarcasm. 'Providing three meals a day for eight men—and the occasional visitor like you—tends to mean that you spend a lot of time in the kitchen.'

She was rather pleased with the subtle way she had managed to dismiss him as an 'occasional visitor'. It made her feel better to remember that he was just passing through, while she had every intention of staying for ever.

'You certainly seem to work very hard,' Guy agreed. 'I'd say a day out is the least you deserve. I quite like the idea of a local rodeo as the outback equivalent of going to the ball, don't you?' he said, with one of those smiles that Lucy was sure was meant to have her swooning with delight. 'Hal gets to be the fairy godmother who says you can go, the stockmen's old truck is the pumpkin that brought you here...now all you need is a Prince Charming!'

He made a show of patting his pockets. 'You know, I'm sure I had a glass slipper somewhere...'

'I've already found my Prince Charming,' said Lucy crushingly, and looked pointedly across the ring to where Kevin was watching a snorting stallion being coaxed into the chute. 'You just get to be an ugly sister,' she said.

To her annoyance, Guy's good humour wasn't even dented, let alone crushed by her dismissive comment. He just laughed, and she sucked her teeth in irritation. Prince Charming indeed! Of course, he *would* think that was his role. The man was unbelievably conceited. Yes, he was remarkably handsome—even she couldn't deny that—but that smooth, blond, blue-eyed look didn't do it for her. She preferred her men rather more rugged.

Like Kevin, in fact.

'I didn't realise that you were coming today,' she said frostily as she turned back to the arena.

'Hey, the ugly sisters always get to have a good time,' he reminded her. 'And rodeos are always fun—to watch, anyway,' he added as the stallion made short work of bucking the latest rider off his back. Guy winced as he hit the ground with a thud. 'Ouch,' he said. 'It's something different, too,' he went on. 'We don't get a lot of rodeos at home, do we?'

Lucy hated the way he said 'we' like that, as if they had something in common. He was always doing that, reminding her—and everyone else—that she was English too and didn't really belong out here any more than he did.

She had been having such a lovely time at Wirrindago. Employed as a cook-cum-housekeeper, she had been thrilled by the isolation and the fact that the men still found horses the easiest way to move around the wild country. It was all so different from the way she had grown up in England, and she had been quite carried away by the romance of it all.

Until Guy had turned up.

Lucy wasn't used to not liking people but from the moment Guy had strolled into the kitchen a few days ago and introduced himself with that smile—the one that seemed to assume that any woman on the receiving end would instantly swoon at his feet—her normally sunny nature had deserted her. There was just something about him that rubbed her up the wrong way, leaving her irritated and edgy.

Guy might be Hal Granger's cousin, but it was hard to imagine anyone more different or more out of place in the outback. He was so…so…so *English,* Lucy decided in frustration. He just didn't belong, and she wished he would go back to London and stop getting on her nerves.

The way he was doing right now.

'I wouldn't have thought rodeos were your kind of thing,' she said.

'Oh, I don't know…' Casually, Guy leant on the rails next

to her. The sleeves of his pristine white shirt were rolled up to reveal surprisingly powerful forearms, covered with a fuzz of golden hairs that drew Lucy's eyes in spite of herself as they glinted in the bright light. There was something over-whelming about him when he was that close, and she found herself edging away.

'I spent quite a lot of holidays at Wirrindago when I was a kid,' he was saying, apparently oblivious to her unease. 'I remember coming to rodeos like this one with Hal. They used to lay on bareback sheep riding and catching the greasy pig for the youngsters.'

He grinned at the memory and she glimpsed a flash of strong white teeth in his brown, too-handsome face. 'We had some good fun. I used to want to be like those guys over there,' he went on, nodding to where the stockmen taking part in the rodeo were sitting on the rails looking for all the world like extras in a classic Western. 'I told my parents I wanted to be a rodeo rider when I left school.'

Lucy stared at him. *'A rodeo rider?'* His shirt was daz-zlingly white in the glare, and she could see the riders on the rails reflected in his sunglasses. There was a sheen to him, she thought, a kind of glamour that belonged on a yacht in St Tropez or skiing off piste in Gstaad, not here at a ramshackle local rodeo with bull-riding and steer-wrestling and greasy pigs. *'You?'*

Still leaning on the rail, Guy glanced up at her with another of those film-star smiles. 'Funny, that's exactly what my fa-ther said—and he said it in just that tone of voice too!'

Lucy wished he would stop smiling like that. It was too much. *He* was too much. Too vibrant. Too good-looking. Too charming. Too everything. She looked away, annoyed to find that the smile seemed to have been imprinted on her vision so that it was just as vivid even when she wasn't looking at him.

'What did your mother say?'

'She told me not to be so silly.'

His imitation of his mother's crisp tones was no doubt wickedly accurate and, in spite of her determination not to find him the slightest bit amusing, Lucy was betrayed into a laugh, which she tried to cover by adjusting the old stockman's hat on her head. She had borrowed it that morning and it was a little big, but it made her feel authentic, unlike Guy Dangerfield, smile or no smile. He might have a closer connection to the outback than she did, but at least she tried to fit in. He just stuck out like the proverbial sore thumb.

'I'm surprised you're not having a go today if you were that keen,' she said.

'I know better now,' said Guy. 'I leave the hard stuff to the experts like Prince Charming over there.'

He nodded across the ring to where Kevin was sitting on the rails, looking quietly confident as another wild horse pawed the ground in the chute, impatient for release into the ring. 'You need to be tough to take on bareback bronc riding.'

'I know,' said Lucy, deciding to ignore the Prince Charming jibe. 'Kevin says it's the supreme rodeo challenge,' she was unable to resist adding. She was at that stage of infatuation when just saying Kevin's name was a thrill.

'Kevin *said* something?' Guy straightened from the rail in mock astonishment. 'When? I didn't know he could talk!'

'Very funny,' said Lucy coldly.

'You've got to admit that he's not exactly chatty,' he said. 'I've hardly heard him say a word at meals since I arrived. I mean, we all know about strong silent types, but that's ridiculous!'

'There's nothing ridiculous about Kevin,' Lucy flared up. 'He just doesn't say anything unless it's worth saying. It's one of the things that makes him a real man—unlike some,' she added pointedly.

Guy leant back against the fence and folded his arms, but Lucy was sure that behind those stupid sunglasses, his eyes were dancing.

'So you think a real man incapable of making conversation?'

'No, he just doesn't waste his time spouting stupid rubbish—like giving people silly nicknames, for instance!'

'Cinders, are you by any chance implying that you don't think *I* am a real man?' Guy tsk-tsked. 'I'm hurt!'

If Lucy had believed for a moment that he had been really offended she would have been embarrassed, but, as it was, she just lifted her chin at him.

'You're not like Kevin,' she said.

'Apart from the fact that I can string more than three words together at a time, what's the real difference between us?'

'Kevin's tough,' said Lucy. 'He's steady, he's sensible and he works hard.' Belatedly, she realised that she hadn't made him sound much fun, and she waited for Guy to point it out, but he only grinned.

'How do you know you couldn't say the same thing about me?'

She eyed him with frustration. Surely he must know how frivolous and superficial he appeared next to someone like Kevin? 'You don't seem to take anything very seriously,' she said at last. 'Do you even have a job?'

'Of course I do!' He pretended to sound affronted. 'I'm in investment banking.'

'Oh...*banking*,' said Lucy disparagingly. 'That's not a real job.'

'Hey, it's not all late lunches and corporate jollies, you know!'

'How did you get into banking?'

Guy smiled crookedly. 'I have to admit that it's a family firm.'

Just as she'd thought. No doubt he'd been given a token job

with a plush office to sit in while everyone else did all the work, Lucy decided. He probably rolled up at ten and spent most of the day at lunch catching up with pals on the old boys' network.

'I don't think you can compare working in a bank with what Kevin does,' she said, determinedly unimpressed. 'You don't need the same kind of skills.'

'Maybe,' said Guy, 'but what can Kevin do that I can't?'

'Well…he's a brilliant horseman.' Lucy had never, in fact, seen Kevin on a horse. As Guy had pointed out, she was usually in the kitchen when the stockmen were at work, but she had heard them talking about how good Kevin was often enough.

'I can ride.'

'I don't mean English riding.'

'*English* riding?' Guy raised his brows, a smile hovering around his mouth, and she gestured irritably.

'You know what I mean. Just sitting on the back of the horse and pottering along a country lane. I'm talking about real horsemanship—working with the horse, being able to control it absolutely the way Kevin can. Taming a wild horse, or bringing down a cow without hurting it…all the things he does every day.'

'I admit I don't spend a lot of time on horseback in the bank, but that doesn't mean I couldn't be a stockman if I wanted. Could Kevin run an investment bank, do you think?'

Lucy looked at him suspiciously. 'Are you really telling me that you can ride like Kevin?'

'I'm not saying I'm any good, I'm just saying that I could be a real man if I wanted to.'

As usual, his face was poker straight, but his voice held that undercurrent of amusement that so riled Lucy. She didn't believe a word of it. He was just teasing her, probably miffed because she thought that Kevin was more of a man.

Lucy's chin went up. She had had enough of being teased by Guy over the last few days. 'Prove it,' she said.

'Prove that I can ride?' Guy rubbed his jaw, a smile tugging at the corner of his mouth. 'Short of throwing myself on to a spare horse, I'm not sure how I can do that.'

'We're at a rodeo,' she pointed out sweetly. 'There are plenty of horses back there.' She nodded in the direction of the holding pens behind the makeshift arena. 'You could take part in one of the competitions.'

'Have you seen those horses?' Guy made a comic face. 'Half of them are completely wild!'

Lucy shrugged. 'You said you could ride,' she reminded him.

'Well, there's riding and riding, if you know what I mean.'

'You're the one who said you could ride like Kevin. I don't think it would be easy, but a real man would like a challenge. You obviously don't,' she finished dismissively, and then regretted it because Guy had straightened and suddenly he seemed very solid and very close.

For one frozen moment she thought she might have gone too far, but then he smiled. Taking off his sunglasses, he looked directly into Lucy's hostile eyes. 'I wouldn't say that, Cinderella,' he said softly.

Lucy had the strangest impression that the noise and smells of the rodeo had faded around them while blue eyes locked with blue. Hers were the blue of a summer sky, while Guy's were darker, a deep ocean blue where laughter lurked like sunlight glinting on the water and, as she stared up at him, held against her will by their gleaming depths, she was suddenly acutely aware of him.

Ever since he had arrived, she had dismissed Guy as a playboy, too handsome for his own good, too charming to be real, but now, all at once, she saw him as a man. A man with warm brown skin and a hint of golden stubble, with a strong jaw and a slightly crooked nose and laughter lines creasing those blue, blue eyes, and something turned over inside her at the realisation that he was not only a very real man but that he was very close.

'In fact,' Guy went on, and his voice held that disturbing undercurrent of amusement and something else that sent a tiny shiver down Lucy's spine, 'I'd say that I enjoy a challenge just as much as the next man, if not more.'

Swallowing, Lucy succeeded in wrenching her gaze away from his at last and she took a step back. 'You'll do it, then?' she said a little unsteadily. She felt odd, as if the ground had been cut away beneath her feet somehow.

Guy grinned again and, in spite of herself, her pulse gave a little kick. 'You know it would be much easier if you would just believe me.'

'I'll believe you when you take part in the next round. It's calf roping next, so they'll give you a proper horse.'

'Calf-roping? You couldn't pick something a bit harder?' said Guy humorously. 'That means I've not only got to stay on the horse but catch a calf with a lasso.'

'It'll be a challenge,' Lucy agreed. 'And according to you, you like one of those!'

'Ah, well, if that's what it takes to convince you, I suppose I'd better—' He broke off as an 'ooooh' came from the crowd standing around the ring. 'Isn't that Kevin?'

'Kevin?' Lucy turned sharply to see Kevin rolling free of the horses' hooves in a little cloud of dust, but he was smiling broadly as he stood up and helped the men catch the horse that was still bucking furiously around the edge of the ring. People were clapping too, so presumably he had stayed on the horse's back for longer than the others.

She had missed his moment of glory. Lucy was mortified, and furious with Guy for distracting her. When Kevin dodged his way across the ring towards her, she gave him a dazzling smile that pointedly excluded Guy.

'You did brilliantly,' she said, trusting that he had been too busy clinging on to the horse to notice that she'd been talking to Guy instead of watching him.

'Wasn't bad,' said Kevin laconically.

'Congratulations,' said Guy, muscling in where he wasn't wanted, as usual. Anyone with any sensitivity would have murmured an excuse and slipped away to leave her alone with Kevin, but not Guy! No, he was right there, shaking Kevin's hand, being friendly and interested and asking him about the skills he needed to stay in the saddle so long, until Kevin was getting positively loquacious.

'Isn't it time you went and got ready for the calf-roping, Guy?' Lucy interrupted as a megaphone crackled into life with an announcement about the next competition. 'You don't want to miss your chance to have a go, do you?'

'You going in for that, Guy?' asked Kevin and she couldn't help noticing that he seemed more interested in that than in anything she had had to say.

'So it seems,' he said, smiling. 'Lucy's issued a challenge that I can't refuse, although I'm not sure that I'll be able to take part. I wouldn't blame the organisers if they didn't want amateurs messing up their competition.'

Lucy wasn't going to let him weasel out of it that easily. 'At least you can go and see.'

Kevin looked puzzled as Guy strolled off. 'I didn't know he could use a rope,' he said.

'He can't,' she said scornfully. 'He's just calling my bluff. You wait, he'll be back in a minute with some excuse about why he can't do it.'

But Guy didn't come back. Lucy should have been perfectly happy now that she was alone with Kevin, but her attention kept being distracted by the laughter from where all the contestants were gathered. Whenever she glanced over, she could see Guy, clowning around, pretending to get on a horse the wrong way round, borrowing a hat, making everybody laugh.

What a show off the man was! Lucy turned her eyes determinedly back to Kevin's ruggedly handsome profile, but it was hard to concentrate with Guy playing to the crowd like that.

The sooner this farce was over, the better, she decided, and was relieved when it seemed to be Guy's turn. They had found him a horse. Someone would give him a boost into the saddle, he could hold on long enough to go round the ring, and she supposed she would have to give him credit for having tried when—

Oh.

Fully expecting him to bungle mounting his horse, Lucy was taken aback when Guy swung easily into the saddle in one fluid movement. Astounded, she watched him manoeuvre his horse behind the barrier and wait while the calf was released from the chute and given a ten second start.

Alarmed by the unfamiliar surroundings, the calf blundered round and round the makeshift arena, looking for a way out until the barrier was raised, and Guy spurred his horse forward, keeping pace with the animal at an easy canter.

Lucy watched, blue eyes gathering wrath as he rode with effortless grace, detaching the lasso from the pommel and testing its weight in his hand as easily as if he had spent his whole life in the saddle.

I can ride. He had told her, but she hadn't believed him. He had known that she wasn't going to believe him, and so he had let her think that he was joking. And now there he was, twirling the rope experimentally before sending it snaking through the air to land neatly over the calf's horns.

Around the ring there was a burst of applause and Guy was instantly in showman mode again, grinning and waving his hat to acknowledge the cheers.

'Not bad for a Pom,' said Kevin.

'No,' said Lucy tightly. Logically, she knew that Guy couldn't possibly have set her up to make a fool of herself, but that was how it felt.

'Come on,' she said abruptly, having had enough of Guy Dangerfield for one afternoon. 'Let's go and find the others.'

'Might as well dump our swags too,' said Kevin. 'There should still be some space down by the creek. That's where we usually sleep.'

It was a long speech for him, but that wasn't why Lucy stopped and looked at him blankly. 'Sleep?'

'There's always a party after the rodeo,' he said as if everybody knew that. 'We have a few beers and there's a dance. Nobody wants to drive home after that.'

'But…I didn't realise you'd be staying.' Lucy regarded him with dismay. 'I promised Hal I'd be back tonight,' she tried to explain. 'His niece and nephew are coming tomorrow and I said I'd help him make sure everything was ready.'

Kevin couldn't see the problem. 'Hal knows you're with us. He won't expect you back until tomorrow.'

She bit her lip uncertainly. 'Did you bring a swag for me?'

'Sure did,' said Kevin and he smiled his slow smile, the one that usually had her heart doing handsprings.

For once, Lucy was too torn to respond. She had longed and longed to spend more time with Kevin, and now, at last, when he seemed to be showing a bit more interest, she wasn't going to be able to enjoy it. It was so unfair.

If only she *could* stay. She loved a good party, and tonight would probably be great fun. There would be a barbecue and dancing in the woolshed and later, perhaps, she and Kevin could slip away down to the creek in the starlight… It could be the perfect romantic evening.

How could it be perfect, though, when she had promised Hal she would go back? She would spend the whole time feeling guilty.

Her boss wasn't the easiest of men and, truth to tell, Lucy was a little intimidated by him, but it was Hal who had given her the job and a chance to work in the outback. If it hadn't been for him, she would never even have met Kevin. And Hal had made it clear that her priority would be looking after his sister's children during their stay at Wirrindago. Lucy had signed a stringent contract to that effect but, even if she hadn't, she wouldn't have wanted to let him down. She owed him too much.

But how could she insist that Kevin drive her back tonight? The other stockmen would have to come too, as they only had the one truck, and they would all miss the party. They had few enough social occasions to look forward to, Lucy knew. It wouldn't be fair to them.

She had promised Hal. It wouldn't be fair to him *not* to go.

'I don't know what to do, Kevin,' she said helplessly. 'I'd love to stay, honestly I would, but I did say that I would go back tonight. If I'd known…'

It was at that moment that Guy came strolling up, as pristine as ever. It looked as if he had hardly broken a sweat on that horse in the crushing heat. Lucy eyed him with deep resentment. He could at least have had the decency to fall off. At least then he would look dirty and normal like everyone else.

As it was, she was convinced with no justification whatsoever that the mess she had found herself in was somehow his fault.

'Satisfied, Cinders?' he asked with a glinting smile.

Lucy gritted her teeth. 'Yes,' she said tersely.

'You were good,' said Kevin. 'You going in for anything else?'

Guy shook his head. 'I'm challenged out,' he said with an amused glance at Lucy. 'I thought I'd head back to Wirrindago now. Hal could do with a bit of support. For a man who can move a thousand head of cattle around without a blink, he seems unnerved by the thought of two children. But I can't say I blame him!'

'Maybe Guy would give you a lift back, Lucy,' said Kevin, and Guy lifted an eyebrow at Lucy in surprise.

'Aren't you staying for the ball, Cinders?'

'It's not a ball.' Kevin was bemused. 'It's just a party.'

Lucy was too disappointed to explain. She knew he was only trying to help, but he hadn't even *tried* to persuade her to stay, and now he was going to offload her on to Guy Dangerfield, of all people!

'I told Hal I'd be back tonight,' she admitted to Guy, almost choking on the words. 'I didn't realise that everyone else would be staying.'

'I'm sure Hal would understand if you wanted to go to the party,' said Guy, who appeared to be able to read her expression without difficulty. 'It's not like you'll really be reduced to rags if you're here after midnight! I'll tell him what's happened, and Kevin can bring you back with the others tomorrow morning.'

'It's all right, thank you,' said Lucy, frigidly polite. She had no intention of enjoying a romantic evening courtesy of Guy, even if she *had* been sure that Kevin would think to take her down to the creek in the starlight. He certainly didn't seem to be making any effort to persuade her to stay, she thought glumly. Perhaps he didn't like her as much as she had hoped?

'I made a promise,' she said, 'and I'll keep it.'

'Good girl.' Guy nodded approvingly. 'I can't say I'd mind having some company on the way back,' he added. 'It's a long drive on your own. The pumpkin's ready whenever you are, Cinders.'

Lucy cast a last longing look at the woolshed. Tonight it would be throbbing with music and laughter, and the old wooden floor would reverberate with dancing feet. The smell of beer would mingle with the smoke from the barbecue, and the light would spill out through the great doors into the vast, silent outback night. It would be the kind of party she had always dreamed of.

And she wouldn't be there. Kevin would be dancing with a nice Australian girl who could talk horses with him, and she would be stuck with the only Englishman for hundreds of miles around. She could have wept with disappointment, but she had given her word to Hal and there was nothing she could do about it now.

She sighed. 'I'm ready now,' she said.

CHAPTER TWO

IT WAS a silent drive at first. To Lucy's relief, Guy didn't try to make conversation. If she hadn't already decided that he was unbearably arrogant and conceited, she might have thought that he was being sensitive about her disappointment. He didn't tease her about not going to the ball, as she had half expected that he would, but let her stare miserably out of the window and think about Kevin and all the other girls he might be dancing with in the woolshed that night.

With a sigh, she took off her hat and ran her fingers through her flattened hair so that it fell, blonde and dishevelled now, to her shoulders. Glancing at Guy under her lashes, she saw that he was watching her with an unreadable expression and, for some reason, she found herself blushing.

'You know, you could have stayed,' he said. 'Hal would have understood.'

'I know, but I'd given him my word.' Aware that she was being self-indulgent, Lucy made an effort to pull herself together. None of this was actually Guy's fault, she realised, and he was her employer's cousin. It might be a little late to start being polite, but she could always try. 'I'm sorry, I'm not being much company,' she said and mustered a smile. 'I'm not usually this miserable.'

'I know,' said Guy. 'I've been struck by what an extraordinarily happy person you are. Most girls your age would
grumble about being stuck in an isolated homestead all day
with nothing to do but cook and clean for a bunch of taci-
turn men and nowhere to go in the evenings, but you seem
to love it.'

'I do love it.' Lucy was surprised that he thought that there
was anything odd about it. 'It's all so romantic! Exactly how
I always imagined the outback to be! I can't believe how
lucky I am to be here.'

'It's just that you give the impression of being a girl who likes
to have fun,' he said, his eyes on the dirt track that ran arrow
straight through the red dust to the horizon. 'I could see how
disappointed you were not to be able to go to the party tonight.'

Lucy eyed him uncertainly, not quite sure how to take him
when he wasn't making fun of her. 'I do love a party, but I
don't mind the isolation.'

She didn't mind anything as long as Kevin was there. If
he'd been beside her instead of Guy, she wouldn't have given
two hoots about the party. As it was, she couldn't help wondering who he was with and what he was doing.

'Maybe living so quietly makes you appreciate social events
more,' she said. 'I'm glad I didn't have to make all the men
come back with me. They don't get to go out much, and they'll
have a great time. It won't matter to them if I'm there or not.'

Guy cast her a glance, evidently not in the least fooled by
her bright smile. 'Kevin isn't going to get together with anyone else tonight, if that's what's worrying you,' he said.

'How can you know?' Lucy abandoned the pretence that
she wasn't worried.

'Hey, Prince Charming never settles for anyone less than
Cinderella, right?'

Lucy wasn't reassured. 'There might be someone more

suitable there.' She turned the hat wistfully in her hands. 'I wish I wasn't so *English*,' she confessed in a low voice.

'Come on,' said Guy as the truck juddered over a rough patch in the track. 'Kevin may not be the most talkative guy in the world, but he's a man, and you're a very pretty girl, as I'm sure you must know. He's not going to be interested in *suitable* when he's got you.'

'I hope you're right,' she said, chewing anxiously at the side of her thumb. 'It's hard to tell with Kevin,' she went on in a burst of confidence, even though part of her was marvelling that she was actually talking to Guy—*Guy*, of all people!—like this.

It must be something about being shut up together in the front seat of the truck, she decided. The cab made for an oddly intimate environment, especially when you were driving across the outback and there was nothing to distract you and no one else around for miles and miles and miles. There wasn't much else to do but talk.

'I just don't know what he feels about me.' She sighed.

'It's hard to tell with someone like Kevin, I agree,' said Guy. 'Not like you.'

'What do you mean?'

'You're obviously not a believer in keeping your feelings to yourself,' he said with a touch of irony. 'It's not very British of you, but I kind of like it.'

Lucy flushed. 'I'm in love with Kevin,' she said, and her glance held more than a hint of defiance. 'Why should I try and deny it?'

'No reason,' said Guy mildly.

'My sister thinks you ought to keep everything bottled up inside,' she went on, a little deflated by his lack of response. 'But if you love someone, why not say it? Why should you be ashamed of your feelings?'

'You shouldn't,' he said, 'but sometimes it's worth keeping

them to yourself until you're absolutely sure that *is* how you feel.'

'You sound like Meredith.' Lucy hunched a shoulder. 'I *am* sure how I feel about Kevin. Why shouldn't I be?'

Guy shrugged. 'You don't need to justify yourself to me,' he pointed out. 'Kevin seems a nice enough bloke, even if he hasn't got much to say for himself. I just wonder how much fun you'll have with him. I mean, what do you talk about when you're together?'

Lucy didn't want to admit that she was rarely alone with Kevin. The Wirrindago homestead might be isolated in the middle of a million acres but there was surprisingly little privacy. The stockmen worked together, ate in the homestead together and then retired to their communal quarters. It was hard to find an opportunity to slip off on your own, or rather with someone else, but if anything, that had only made Lucy yearn for Kevin even more.

She had fallen in love with him on her first evening at Wirrindago. He had walked on to the veranda, a dream come true in his checked shirt and boots and rugged male attraction, and Lucy had been lost. He was perfect, her dream of living forever in the outback with him was perfect, and she didn't want Guy Dangerfield casting doubt on it.

'When you're really in love, nothing else matters,' she said loftily. 'It's not about making conversation. It's about being together and loving each other.'

'If you say so,' said Guy, clearly unconvinced. 'It can be a lonely life in the outback, though.'

'Not if I'm with Kevin.' Lucy was uncomfortably aware that she was making her relationship with Kevin seem rather more established than it was, but it was a point of principle more than anything else. 'You dreamed about being a rodeo rider,' she said. 'Well, this is *my* dream.'

She shook back her hair defiantly, and Guy sent her a sideways glance.

'I grew out of that particular fantasy,' he pointed out. 'About…oooh…eighteen years ago.'

'And have you never had a fantasy since?'

As soon as the words were out, Lucy wished that she had phrased it differently. She saw the corner of Guy's mouth twitch, and she felt a flush creeping up her cheeks at the unwitting suggestiveness of her question. 'You know what I mean,' she snapped. 'A dream. You're not going to tell me that you don't dream any more, are you?'

'No.'

Lucy half turned in her seat, suddenly curious. Guy might give the impression of being very open and friendly, but behind that lazily good-humoured expression it was hard to know what he really felt about anything.

'So what do you dream about now, if it's not rodeo riding?' she asked.

Guy's smile gleamed. 'I don't think I know you well enough to tell you that, Lucy,' he said. 'I'm with your sister on that one, I have to admit. Some fantasies are best kept to oneself!'

Lucy gripped her tongue between her teeth as she smeared chocolate icing over the top of the cake. Ostensibly it was for afternoon smoko, but really she had made it for Kevin. Chocolate cake was his favourite, so she made it as often as she could.

She was feeling very happy today. Kevin had actually said that he had missed her at the party after the rodeo, and Lucy hugged the memory of his laconic comment to her as if it had been the most passionate declaration of love. A man like Kevin wasn't going to rush into anything, she reminded herself frequently, so admitting that he had missed her was a big step.

It was a start, anyway.

Even better, Guy Dangerfield was leaving at last. His mother was having a double hip replacement, he had explained, and he needed to fly back to London the next day so that he could be around to help her after the operation.

Lucy would be relieved to see him go. It wasn't that he had been about the place that much. If anything, she had seen less of him since that drive back from the rodeo, but she had been uncomfortably aware of him at meals, when his smile kept snagging at the edge of her vision, and his voice with its undercurrent of laughter was somehow impossible to ignore, even if he was talking at the other end of the table.

She wished she hadn't told him quite so much about herself, although Guy had never mentioned their conversation again. At odd times, Lucy would find herself thinking about how he had looked on that drive, and remembering things that she hadn't even been aware of noticing at the time.

Like his hands, strong and square on the steering wheel, or the line of his jaw. Like the texture of his skin, his throat brown above the white collar. Like the curl of his mouth and the gleam of his smile.

And then she would remember how easily he had swung on to that horse and a strange feeling would uncurl in the pit of her stomach.

It all made her feel very unsettled. Lucy tried reminding herself how irritating he had been, and the annoying way he would insist on calling her Cinderella, and she told herself she was glad that he didn't come into the kitchen to chat any more, but she couldn't help feeling just a little piqued when he just waved a greeting on his way past and left her alone.

Wondering why she should care at all just made her more unsettled. It was a very good thing that Guy was going, she decided as she put the finishing touches to the cake. Tomorrow she would be able to relax at last, without the constant distraction of Guy's presence, and maybe there would be a chance to spend more time with Kevin.

Not that there was any time to spend on building a quality relationship at the moment. Hal's sister had brought her children, Emma and Mickey, to stay before flying out to join her husband on a two-month business tour, and they were having a hard time adjusting.

Lucy felt sorry for them. She knew what it was like to be homesick, having been sent to boarding school at seven, but she had had her big sister, Meredith, to look after her. Emma, at nine, didn't seem nearly as practical as Meredith, or as devoted to looking after her younger brother, so Lucy was doing her best to keep them entertained in between making sure there were meals on the table three times a day.

Right now, the two of them were on the front veranda, playing some computer game, but she would go and suggest they play a game of cards or something as soon as she had cleared up the kitchen.

Brushing cocoa from her jeans, she glanced at the kitchen clock. Hal should be back soon. He had driven into Whyman's Creek earlier that morning and she had given him a whole list of ingredients to pick up from the store.

Lucy put the cake to one side and regarded the mess she had made with a sigh. She was an exuberant cook and she had never got the hang of washing up as she went along. She always put off the moment of tidying up as long as she could.

'Uncle Hal's here!'

Emma's cry from the front veranda made Lucy brighten at the perfect excuse to avoid tackling the mess for a while. Wiping her hands on a tea towel, she hurried along the corridor to help Hal unload.

The front door stood open, but a screen door kept out the

insects. It fell into place with a clatter after Lucy exited and
made for the steps leading down to where Hal had parked the
truck. She saw his tall figure first, and then noticed with surprise that he had brought someone with him. He hadn't said
anything about a visitor when he left that morning.

Lucy's blue gaze was on its way back to Hal when it
stopped and returned to the stranger in a ludicrous double
take. Surely not? It *couldn't* be…?

But it was. Her sister, so dearly familiar and yet so utterly
unexpected out here that for a long, long moment, Lucy could
only stare.

Meredith?

Meredith looked up at her. 'Hi, Lucy,' she said.

It *was* her! Lucy's heart swelled with astonished delight.
She hadn't realised how much she had missed her no-
nonsense sister until now. Hurrying down the steps, she swept
Meredith into a hug.

'I can't believe it's really you!' she cried excitedly. 'It's *so*
good to see you!' Then she pulled back to look into her sister's
face. 'But what on *earth* are you doing here?'

'Your *sister?*' Guy's brows rose. He had been out all day and
had only just come back to discover that Hal had brought an
unexpected visitor back from Whyman's Creek. 'Has she
come out to visit you?'

'Not exactly.' Lucy was distracted as she turned the
potatoes in the hot fat.

They needed more cold meat for lunchtime sandwiches,
so she had planned to roast another huge joint tonight and now
she was glad. She could cook roast beef in her sleep these
days, and she had too much on her mind to concentrate on
anything more complicated.

'She wants me to go home with her,' she told Guy. 'A

friend of ours has been in an accident. He's in a coma, and they think that my voice might help him to come round.'

Guy sat on the kitchen table and regarded Lucy's downcast face thoughtfully. 'That's bad news.'

Lucy sighed, too miserable even to resent Guy's presence. 'I know.'

'What are you going to do?'

'I think I'm going to have to go,' she said. 'It would mean breaking my contract—you know how insistent Hal was that I was here to look after Emma and Mickey—but Meredith's talking to him now and we're hoping that he'll agree to her taking my place while I go back to London and see Richard.'

Guy frowned slightly. 'Will it really make such a difference if you're there?'

'Meredith seems to think that it will.' Lucy put the potatoes back into the oven and straightened, smoothing some stray hairs from her forehead with the back of her arm. 'To be honest, I don't want to go, but I owe Meredith a lot and if this is what she wants, then I'll do what I can. I spoke to Richard's mother on the phone, too. She sounded desperate, as if they've pinned all their hopes on me going back. How can I refuse when it means so much to them?'

Guy hesitated. 'What about Kevin?'

'He'll wait for me, I hope,' she said, her eyes sliding away from his. 'Even if Hal doesn't agree to keep the job open for me if Meredith stays, then I'll get back to the outback somehow. I'm not going to just give up on my dream.'

But Hal had agreed, Meredith told her, when she came into the kitchen a little later and was introduced to Guy.

'Now we just need to get you to Darwin,' she told Lucy.

'I can help you there,' said Guy. 'As it happens, your timing couldn't be better.' He told Meredith about his mother's hip operation. 'I need to be there,' he said, 'not that Ma will appreciate it! She'll probably just tell me that I'm in the way, but I've chartered a plane to pick me up from the airstrip here tomorrow morning anyway. The pilot will fly me directly to Darwin, and I can pick up the London flight there. Lucy might as well come with me.'

Lucy had been listening to him with growing dismay, but Meredith's face lightened. 'That would be great,' she said gratefully. 'It means she can get home much sooner.'

'I'm sure we can find a local flight,' Lucy cut across her. 'We don't need to put Guy to any trouble.'

'It's no trouble,' said Guy. 'There's room for another person on the plane and, as I've chartered it, it won't cost any extra.' He glanced at Lucy's mutinous face. 'Of course, the alternative is for Hal to drive you into Whyman's Creek,' he said mildly. 'There's a local flight to Darwin and you might be able to get a seat on it, but as Hal's just got back from town today, he'd probably be glad not to have to drive you in again tomorrow morning.'

This was so patently true that Lucy was left with nothing to say, as Guy was no doubt perfectly aware. She could hardly insist on Hal going to all the effort of driving her into town on the off chance she would get a seat on the next flight when it had taken all Meredith's persuasive powers to get him to agree to her leaving at all.

Raging inwardly at the workings of fate, Lucy threw her things into her rucksack the next morning. She had so been looking forward to Guy going, and to spending some time alone with Kevin—well, without Guy's smile lurking distractingly in the background, anyway—and now here she was, leaving with him instead of waving him off with a bright smile. Spending an hour and a half alone with him on the drive back from the rodeo had been bad enough. How was she going to manage going all the way to Darwin?

They were even going to be on the same plane to London, she had discovered to her dismay. While she had been saying goodbye to Kevin, Guy had been on the phone, arranging her ticket.

'Meredith said she would do that,' Lucy protested when she found out, but Guy only shrugged.

'Meredith was exhausted last night,' he pointed out. 'It seemed the important thing was to get you on to the first plane so I got my PA to book you on the same flight.'

At least she would only have to put up with him until they got to Darwin, Lucy consoled herself. Guy was a first class traveller if ever she saw one, and she was most definitely a budget traveller. Once they got to Darwin, he would be so coddled by special lounges and fast track service that with any luck she wouldn't see him again after that.

But there was another shock at Darwin itself. 'You've booked me in first class?' Lucy's voice rose to a squeak of appalled dismay.

'It's a long flight,' said Guy. 'You might as well be comfortable.'

'Meredith told me that Richard's parents wanted to buy my ticket home, but I'm quite sure they didn't intend me to come first class!' Lucy was aghast. 'I know Richard's father is a successful businessman, but he's not so successful he can afford to hand out first class plane tickets.'

'In that case, it's lucky that I am,' said Guy, putting a firm hand under her elbow and piloting her towards the first class check-in desk. 'Richard's parents can pay for your ticket back to Australia, and you can travel as economically as you like then.'

Lucy dug in her heels as she realised what he was saying and rather belatedly wrenched her arm out of his warm grasp. '*You* bought my ticket to London?'

'I can't take any credit for it. My PA did all the work.'

'But I can't let you pay for me. I hardly know you!'

'Oh, I wouldn't say that,' said Guy, repossessing her elbow and propelling her firmly forwards. 'We've been living in the same house for the past week. You know that I like marmalade on my toast and I know that you're not at your best in the mornings. I know how you feel about Kevin, and you know that I once wanted to be a rodeo star. Very few people know that about me, Cinders,' he said with a gleaming smile. 'We can't be strangers when you know my embarrassing secret!'

'But it's so expensive!' said Lucy, hanging back.

'Lucy, I'm a rich man,' he said patiently. 'It won't even be a blip in my bank account.'

And somehow Lucy found herself handing over her passport as Guy checked them both in. The bookings had been made electronically, and in no time at all she was on the plane, with none of the shuffling queues she was used to, and ensconced in a luxurious seat by the window. There was no denying that the whole process of boarding was a lot less stressful in first class.

'Wow,' she said, pushing her seat back and playing with all the buttons, forgetting for a moment that she was cross with Guy. 'I've never been in the pointy end of a plane before. This is great!'

Guy watched her indulgently. 'I've never seen anyone get so much pleasure out of an airline seat,' he said, and Lucy flushed and stopped fiddling immediately. She was obviously being very un-cool.

'I don't suppose you've ever been at the back of the plane.' she grumbled.

'No,' he said. 'Never. I had a very privileged upbringing.'

That accounted for his assurance, anyway. Guy only had to lift an eyebrow for someone to rush to do his bidding.

Lucy would love to have accused him of arrogance but she couldn't. He was charming to everyone, and all the flight attendants, male and female, were soon fawning over him.

Lucy watched them darkly. There was no need for them to lean quite that close to him or smile quite so invitingly, surely? She might as well not have been there! They had obviously taken one look at her jeans and shirt and recognised that she wasn't a first class traveller.

As if to disprove her, a beautifully groomed flight attendant, who made Lucy feel even scruffier than ever, leant past Guy.

'Would you like some champagne, Miss West?'

Miss West! Champagne! Who would ever have thought that she, Lucy West, would be sitting in first class, drinking champagne?

Lucy was ashamed of the little thrill that went through her as she accepted a glass. No flight attendant had ever bothered to learn her name before. She had always just been part of the mass and, while she was perfectly happy being one of a crowd, it was undeniably nice to have all this attention.

She glanced at Guy, who obviously took all this luxury for granted. He raised his glass to her with one of those smiles that always left her feeling slightly ruffled. 'Here's to dreams,' he said.

Lucy thought of Kevin, back at Wirrindago. Even she couldn't pretend that his farewell had been emotional. 'See you then,' he had said as she had left. But outback men weren't used to expressing their emotions, Lucy reminded herself. It didn't mean her dream wouldn't come true.

'To dreams,' she said with a touch of defiance and touched her glass to Guy's. 'May they all come true.'

'I'll drink to that,' said Guy and, as their eyes met for the toast, Lucy found her gaze snared in the gleaming blue depths of his, just as it had done at the rodeo. Just as before, she felt the air shorten between them. There was the same strange fluttery sensation in her stomach, and it made her nervous in exactly the same way.

Lucy yanked her eyes away, feeling oddly breathless, and took a gulp of champagne as she thought longingly of Kevin. Kevin, so quiet, so steady. He never made her feel jangly and jittery like this. You always knew where you were with Kevin. It might not be exactly where you wanted to be, but there was something restful about being able to adore him without expecting much in return.

There was nothing restful about being with Guy. Lucy did her best to ignore him, but it was impossible. If you were used to economy class, the space between the seats was enormous, but still he seemed very close, and she wished that she was sitting behind him or in front of him or anywhere else, in fact, where she might not be quite so aware of him.

He was absorbed in the *Financial Times*, which meant that she could study him covertly as she drank her champagne, and it felt to Lucy as if she had never looked at him properly before. His palely striped shirt was open at the collar and his sleeves were casually rolled up above his wrists. He lounged back in his seat, long legs stretched out before him and crossed at the ankle, utterly relaxed and evidently completely unperturbed by *her* presence.

He was like a big cat, thought Lucy in a flash of revelation, like a golden lion lolling in the shade of an acacia. He had the same air of carelessly leashed power, of a lazy indulgence that could turn in a flash into danger. No wonder he made her nervous. And no wonder he was so little bothered by her.

Guy turned a page of the paper, shaking it straight, and Lucy's eyes snared on his forearm, and for some reason the breath dried in her throat. It was ridiculous. It was just an arm, adorned with what was no doubt an obscenely expensive watch, with broad wrists and square hands, but she was suddenly consumed with the inexplicable need to run her hand along his forearm, to feel the strength of his muscles, the fine golden hairs beneath her palm, the warmth of his skin…

Heat washed through her at the very thought of it and she emptied her glass with a kind of desperation. Her fingers were actually twitching, she realised wildly. Terrified that they might somehow acquire a will of their own and reach out for him, Lucy made herself turn to look out of the window, but there was nothing to see but air and light and the occasional wisp of cloud far below, and the more she stared, the more she saw instead Guy's blue eyes, gleaming with that smile that made her prickle all over.

'More champagne?'

Glad of the distraction, Lucy held out her glass to be refilled. 'It feels all wrong to be drinking champagne in all this luxury when I'm only here because Richard is so ill,' she said to Guy, who lowered his paper with just a hint of reluctance.

Lucy didn't care. He could catch up on what was happening with the Dow-Jones Index some other time. Right now, she wanted him to be annoying. She was counting on it, in fact. She needed him to remind her of everything that she disliked about him so that she would get over this weird and rather embarrassing longing to touch him.

'Will he get better any quicker if you drink water?' asked Guy.

Good, thought Lucy, seizing on what she was sure was a touch of condescension in his voice. 'No…but…you know what I mean,' she said. 'I shouldn't be enjoying myself.'

'This guy you're going back to see…Richard?…presumably everyone wants you to be there because they know he cares about you?'

'Yes,' she acknowledged with some reluctance. She wasn't at all comfortable with the idea that Richard was still in love with her, although Meredith insisted it was true.

'Then I'm prepared to bet that what he likes most about you is your ability to enjoy yourself wherever you happen to be,' said Guy. 'That's what makes you special, Cinders, not your blonde hair and blue eyes, lovely though they are.'

No, that wasn't what she needed him to say at all. Why couldn't he mock her? Why wasn't he teasing her and making her feel stupid, instead of telling her that she was special? Used to the idea that Guy thought she was really rather silly, Lucy was now completely thrown.

'I wish you wouldn't call me Cinders,' she muttered, not knowing what else to say. 'It's stupid.'

'This Richard isn't going to want you to change just because he's ill,' said Guy, ignoring her interjection. 'If anything, he would want you to be even more yourself than usual. It's enough that you're going home when you don't really want to. You don't need to feel guilty as well.'

'But I do,' Lucy blurted out. 'It feels as if it's all my fault that Richard is in such a bad way.'

Guy didn't quite roll his eyes, but there was an exaggerated patience in the way he folded his paper. 'What, you drove the car that put Richard in a coma?'

'No, of course not,' she said, glad to feel a spurt of irritation with him. That was much more like it! 'But I know Meredith thinks that he had the accident because he wasn't concentrating, and he wasn't concentrating because he was upset about me.' She took a morose sip of champagne. 'She hasn't said anything, but I know she blames me for leaving.'

'Ah,' said Guy. 'So you and Richard were more than just friends?'

Lucy nodded. 'But not much more,' she said quickly. 'We

went out for a while, but that's all. It wasn't a big deal. He was a friend of Meredith's and I didn't realise until too late that she was in love with him, but hadn't let on to anyone how she felt. So Richard didn't have a clue, and I didn't either. I would never have gone out with him if I'd known.

'It's not that Richard isn't lovely—he is. He's very intelligent and charming and nice-looking and…steady, I suppose. I'd just broken up with a boyfriend who was the opposite of that. Tom was great fun, but he was wild and unreliable and Richard seemed like a grown-up next to him, so when he asked me out, I couldn't see any reason to say no.'

Guy had turned slightly in his seat to listen to her. 'When did you realise how Meredith felt about him?'

'Not until about a month later.' Lucy turned the champagne flute in her hands, remembering how aghast she had been. 'If only she'd *told* me! But that's typical of Meredith.' She sighed. 'She keeps everything to herself. I only found out by accident. I just happened to see her face in the mirror when I was talking about Richard, and suddenly it was so obvious, I couldn't believe that I hadn't guessed before.'

'It must have been an awkward situation,' commented Guy.

'I felt *awful*.' It was a relief being able to talk to Guy about it, Lucy realised. 'Meredith's my big sister and she's done everything for me. The last thing I wanted was to hurt her. I would *never* have encouraged Richard if I'd known how she felt.'

'So what happened?'

'The honest truth is that Richard and I weren't going anywhere. He's lovely, but a bit serious for me, and we didn't really have much in common, not like him and Meredith. I thought that Richard felt the same way and that the best thing would be for me to leave. If I was out of the way, I was sure they'd get together and everything would be all right.'

Guy glanced at her and his eyes gleamed. 'That was very selfless of you, Lucy.'

Lucy had the grace to blush a little. 'I'm not saying that it didn't suit me. The fact is that I was bored with my job and feeling restless anyway. I'd always loved the idea of the outback and it seemed the perfect opportunity to get a working visa and go.

'That's how I ended up at Wirrindago, and I've been so happy there,' she said with a wistful smile. 'Meredith was furious with me for going, though. She said I'd hurt Richard and that I was being selfish, and things were rather strained between us when I left. I didn't honestly think that Richard was that upset, but she told me yesterday that he was devastated. Apparently he's been confiding in her. She says he still loves me and that's why they all want me to go back now but, to be honest, I felt worse about hurting Meredith.'

Lucy grimaced at the very thought of how unhappy her sister must have been when she'd walked off with Richard under her nose. 'Meredith was known as the sensible one and I was the party girl who never settled down to anything. We lost our mother when we were both small and it was always Meredith who looked after me.'

'It seems to me that she's still doing that,' said Guy. 'And you let her.'

Lucy paused with the champagne glass halfway to her lips. 'What do you mean?'

'Who was it who arranged everything with Hal so that you could go back?' he asked, unfolding his paper once more. 'You didn't even think about booking a flight. You just assumed Meredith would do it for you. And if Meredith isn't around, I'll bet there's always someone else—like me on this occasion—who'll sort things out for you.'

'That's not fair,' she said, but her voice didn't hold quite enough conviction, and Guy glanced at her face before he returned to the *Financial Times*.

'Isn't it?' he said.

CHAPTER THREE

Was that how Guy thought of her? As a lazy brat who let others organise her life for her? Lucy shifted uneasily in her seat. The trouble was that Meredith was so competent that it was often easier to let her do things her own way. But that didn't mean she was spoilt, she thought defensively.

Did it?

A little sulkily, Lucy pulled out the in-flight magazine and began to flick through it mindlessly. The truth was that she didn't like the idea that Guy thought that she was, especially when she had dismissed *him* as a spoilt trust-fund baby at first. There was irony for you.

But it was hard to stay grumpy when you were continually being plied with delicious food and wine and exhorted to lie back and make yourself comfortable, and Lucy's spirits, naturally buoyant, soon rose.

She had never travelled in such style before. She wasn't even bored. The complimentary bag of toiletries was fun to unpack. There were films to watch, magazines to read, a drink on hand whenever she felt like one, and the ultimate luxury of a seat that folded completely flat into a bed. The long flight was an odd kind of limbo time when all she could do was sit there, so Lucy determined that she might as well enjoy doing nothing while she could.

It was only as they began their descent into Heathrow, down through the clouds into a murky London dawn, that her mood began to sink with the plane. It would soon be time to face reality again. She would have to go and see Richard in the hospital, but what if he didn't come out of his coma? She couldn't hang around indefinitely. She didn't have any money and even though Meredith had said that she could live in—

'Oh!' Lucy's hand went to her mouth in an involuntary gesture as she remembered.

'What is it?' Guy stopped in the middle of a long stretch and looked at her dismayed expression in concern.

'It was all such a rush before we left that Meredith forgot to give me the keys to her house!'

'Or perhaps you forgot to ask for them,' he suggested gently.

Lucy opened her mouth to make a sharp retort, but stopped herself just in time. Closing it again, she made herself count to ten. 'Yes,' she agreed through her teeth after a moment, 'you're right, of course. I forgot to remind her about them.'

She sighed. 'I'll have to call round some friends to see if anyone can put me up.' Her shoulders slumped. 'I was dying for a shower, too!'

'It's a bit early to ring round in search of a bed isn't it?' said Guy, glancing at his watch. 'It's not six yet. I can't see you getting many warm invitations to pop straight round at this hour of the morning.'

Lucy made a face. 'I'll try Meg first. She's an old friend.' An old friend who was notoriously grumpy in the mornings. 'She'll forgive me…I hope!'

'Why don't you come back with me?' suggested Guy. 'I've got a car meeting me, and the flat has a couple of spare rooms. You could have a shower and call the hospital and your friends from there.'

'That's kind of you, but I think you've done more than

enough,' said Lucy firmly. She hadn't forgotten his suggestion that she was incapable of looking after herself. She would
show Guy that she could manage perfectly well on her own.
'I'll be fine.'

But when they got to the baggage hall she discovered that
she had no charge on her phone. Lucy sighed. Why did this
kind of thing keep happening to her? She could spend all
morning at Heathrow, trying to contact Meg on a public
phone.

Or she could swallow her pride and ask Guy if she could
take him up on his offer after all.

Lucky she had never been that proud.

Her jaw actually dropped when she saw Guy's apartment.
After first class and the luxury of stepping into a sleek limousine that had pulled up right outside the terminal, she had
thought that she might be getting blasé, but the apartment
block in the heart of London's Docklands was a different
world altogether.

'Home' was too cosy a word for Guy's penthouse, right at
the top of the soaring tower, with heart-stopping three hun-
dred and sixty degree views across London. He had access to
a fabulous bar, a gym, a spa and even a private cinema with
reclining leather seats should he care to see the latest film with
a few friends in comfort.

It could hardly have been more different from the isolated
homestead at Wirrindago. Strange to think that they had been
there only the day before.

'Gosh,' was all she could say when Guy showed her into
his apartment. It was like stepping into something from a
design magazine. The curved wall of the huge living area was
made entirely of glass, opening on to a balcony with a spectacular view over the great bend of the Thames far below. The

floor was of polished oak, and the entire apartment was deco-
rated in cream and neutrals that created a sense of light and
calm.

Lucy wouldn't have been human if she hadn't been impressed, although she did her best not to look too intimidated. The kitchen was all steel and granite and electronic
control panels. 'A bit different from the kitchen at Wirrindago,
isn't it?' she said.

'I believe it was designed by NASA,' said Guy, straight-
faced. 'I get up in the morning and think, What shall I do?
Boil an egg or launch a space shuttle?'

Lucy laughed. 'Do you ever do anything as boring as
cook in it?'

'Nope. Cooking is not one of my talents,' he admitted.

'It seems a shame to have all this and not use it,' she said,
running her hand over the granite worktop.

Guy shrugged. 'I can order in food if I have guests, or there
are plenty of restaurants round here. I tend just to keep the
basics. The housekeeping service should have stocked the
fridge.' He opened the steel door. 'Ah, yes…milk, orange
juice, water… There should be bread and fruit somewhere,
too,' he added as he closed the fridge. 'Help yourself to whatever you want.'

He showed Lucy into a room with a floor to ceiling window looking down on to the river and the vibrant commer-
cial centre that had grown out of the old docks of London.
Even in the dull light, the glass windows of the great towers
glittered as they thrust upwards, and it was hard to imagine
that once great ships had been tied up at the quays and wharfs
that were now home to bars and shops and cafés.

The view was impressive enough, but Lucy actually
gasped when she saw the bathroom. 'This is fabulous!' she
said. 'I'll never dare use it!'

'I thought you were desperate for a shower?'

'I am, but once I'm in there, I may never want to leave. I'd better ring Richard's mother first, anyway,' she said, guiltily remembering why she was there. 'May I use your phone until my mobile is charged up?'

Guy went to have a shower himself while she was talking to Richard's mother, and as he came out of his room a little later he saw Lucy put down the phone with a tiny grimace.

'Bad news?'

'Not really. Richard's much the same, I gather. I can go and see him this afternoon.'

Guy's hair was wet from the shower and he was buttoning up his shirt. The action seemed extraordinarily intimate and Lucy averted her eyes, suddenly self-conscious. 'I'm afraid his mother is expecting miracles, though.'

'In what way?' Barefoot, Guy walked over to the kitchen and filled the kettle. 'Fancy some coffee?'

'That would be wonderful,' said Lucy, subsiding gratefully on to one of the chrome stools at the kitchen bar. In spite of sleeping on the plane, she was suddenly so tired that she thought even coffee wouldn't be able to keep her awake.

She pushed her hair wearily away from her face. 'Ellen seems convinced that Richard will wake up as soon as I open my mouth.' She hesitated. 'I'm hoping they haven't got the wrong idea.'

Guy was wrestling with the coffee machine, which like everything else in the apartment was the latest cutting-edge technology. 'Sometimes I miss instant coffee,' he said with a grunt of frustration. 'At least you didn't need a degree in computer science whenever you wanted a mug of coffee.'

'Let me.' Lucy slid off her stool and went over to push him

out of the way. 'There you go,' she said smugly and, as if by magic, the machine purred into life.

'How did you do that?' Guy stared at her, impressed.

'I worked in a café for a while,' she said, climbing back on to her stool. 'I may not be able to rope a calf, but I can make coffee.'

'Which is, frankly, a lot more useful in Canary Wharf.' Guy opened the fridge again to find milk and orange juice. 'So, what have Richard's parents got the wrong idea about?'

'Ellen seems to be under the impression that I rushed back to see him the moment I heard he was ill because I'm still in love with him,' said Lucy glumly. 'She was talking as if Richard and I will get engaged the moment he wakes up.'

Guy found some glasses and poured two glasses of juice. 'Tell them about Kevin,' he advised. 'If they know you're in love with someone else, they won't waste their time hoping it will all be all right when Richard comes round. It's much better to be honest.'

Lucy brightened. 'Yes, I suppose I could mention Kevin if it starts getting awkward. That's a good idea.' She yawned hugely. 'Sorry, it's all catching up on me.'

'You could have a nap if you don't have to go to the hospital until this afternoon.'

'I might do that after I've rung Meg.' She registered what he was wearing for the first time. 'Are you going to work?' she asked in surprise.

'Of course. We're back in the city now,' said Guy, putting on an air of importance. 'Places to go, things to do, people to see… You know how it is!'

'You probably just want to show off your tan,' she said, a little snip in her voice, and he grinned.

'That too. I'll let you have the door codes,' he told her, 'and then you can come and go as you want.'

* * *

The apartment was empty when Lucy got back from the hospital that evening. She frowned, looking at her watch. Surely Guy wasn't still at the office? He hadn't said he'd be this late.

But then, he hadn't said when he would be back, and why should he? He didn't have to account to her. She was just his cousin's cook, and a man like Guy would no doubt have a scintillating social life to go with his ultra-glamorous apartment. He would be out every night at parties or in clubs, eating in expensive restaurants and mixing with the celebrity A-list.

Lucy looked around at the stylish furniture and minimalist décor. No, this wasn't the kind of apartment you came back to for cosy nights in, to collapse on the sofa after a hard day at work and watch television with a take-away. It was the sort of place you brought your beautiful, sophisticated girlfriend and seduced her with the lights of London at your feet.

Maybe Guy was with that beautiful someone right now. He might be in the middle of a passionate reunion, bemoaning the fact that he couldn't take his girlfriend back to the apartment because it was occupied by someone who wasn't in the slightest bit sophisticated. Lucy looked down at her jeans and T-shirt and only just stopped herself sighing in time.

Of course, she didn't know that he had a girlfriend, but Guy seemed like the kind of man who would always have the prettiest woman on his arm. He hadn't mentioned anyone at Wirrindago, but that didn't mean anything. The conversation around the table there was strictly masculine and didn't include any discussion of emotions or relationships. They could have had a wife and six children apiece for all Lucy would have gathered from their talk.

Lucy helped herself to an apple from the fruit bowl and wandered around the vast living area. She told herself that she

was keeping her mind off how hungry she felt, but the truth
was that she was just being nosy. There were a few photos
out, all in stylish frames, and she picked them up to study
them curiously. She recognised one of Wirrindago, of Guy as
a boy with a much younger-looking Hal. There was a couple
she assumed were his parents, and the odd picture of friends,
sailing or skiing, but definitely no couple shots.

Hmm.

She was holding a photo of Guy as a young man, tanned
and tousle-haired on a surfboard, when the sound of the door
opening made her jump. Quickly, she put the frame down and
turned to see Guy himself. He brought a burst of energy into
the room with him and the apartment, which had seemed so
cold and empty a moment ago, was suddenly alive.

The air seemed to whoosh out of Lucy's lungs at the sight
of him and for a moment she struggled to breathe. He was at
once terrifyingly familiar and yet a stranger in his immaculate
suit and tie. They made him look older, more responsible, even
a little intimidating, and Lucy felt suddenly, ridiculously, shy.

But then his eyes fell on her and he smiled and, having just
remembered how to operate her lungs, she promptly forgot
how to breathe again. He was Guy once more, Guy with those
warm blue eyes and that curling mouth and the laughter in
his voice, Guy who had cantered around the ring on his horse,
testing the lasso in his hand. He had never made her feel
quite like this, though.

'Hello, there,' he said.

'Hi.' Lucy was appalled to hear her voice come out as no
more than a squeak. She cleared her throat and tried again.
'That was a long day at the office after a flight from Australia.
You must be tired.'

'Oh, I wasn't at the office all this time,' said Guy, pulling
at his tie to loosen it.

'I wondered if you might have been catching up with someone special,' said Lucy, ultra casual.

'I was, in fact,' he said. 'Very special.'

'Oh.' It was just as she'd imagined, then. He'd had to tear himself away. *Sorry, darling*, he would have said. *I'll have to go and keep an eye on Lucy. She doesn't seem to have a clue how to look after herself.*

'My mother,' said Guy. 'She's going in for her operation in three days and is nervous about it but, being Ma, she won't admit it. Her temper isn't exactly sweet at the best of times and the pain in her hip is making it worse, so she'd bitten my head off twice before I even got in the door! I was glad to have you as an excuse to leave a bit earlier, I've got to admit.'

'Oh,' said Lucy again, a little unnerved by how relieved she felt. *And what, exactly, are you relieved about, Lucy?* a little voice asked in her head. *Surely not that he chose to visit his mother instead of a girlfriend? Because that would be a very bad sign, given that his love life is absolutely none of your business.*

Oh, and because you're in love with Kevin...remember that?

Guy threw himself down in a chair and stretched his arms above his head. 'How did you get on at the hospital?'

'They say Richard's getting better, but he looked awful to me.' Glad of the change of subject, Lucy sat down opposite him on one of the plush cream sofas. 'He was just lying there, wired up to all these machines. His parents are in a terrible state. They practically fell on my neck when I arrived.'

She sighed at the memory. 'I sat and talked to Richard while they had a break. It felt awkward at first, talking to someone who couldn't reply, so I ended up just saying the first thing that came into my head.'

Not knowing what else to talk about, she had begun by describing Wirrindago and her life there, but somehow she had ended up telling the silent Richard about flying back with Guy, and how unsettled he made her feel.

'It was just rubbish,' she said, faint colour staining her cheeks. 'No wonder he didn't come round! His parents were bitterly disappointed, though, so I said I would go back and try again tomorrow. Of course that just seemed to confirm to them that I had come back for Richard.'

'Did you mention Kevin?'

'Not exactly…' Lucy fingered the piping on a cushion and avoided Guy's eyes. 'I did say that I had a boyfriend, but I wasn't sure that they'd be that convinced if they knew that he was still in Australia, so I thought it would be more convincing if I said that I had come back to London with him.'

She cleared her throat. 'Actually,' she confessed, 'I said it was you.'

Guy had been stretched out comfortably in his chair but at that he brought his arms down sharply and sat up straight.

'You said that *I* was your boyfriend?'

'Well, I said that my boyfriend's name was Guy and that I was staying with him,' said Lucy, uneasily conscious that she might have gone a bit far. 'I didn't think that you would mind. I mean, it doesn't make any difference to you, does it? It's not as if you'll have to *do* anything.'

Guy's expression was quite unreadable and Lucy regarded him doubtfully. It had seemed a good idea at the time, and she hadn't really thought when she had told Richard's parents about him, but perhaps it was a bit of a cheek.

'I'm sorry,' she said uncertainly. 'You obviously *do* mind.'

The unfathomable look in the blue eyes dissolved abruptly and he was smiling once more. 'Of course not,' he said. 'I'm flattered you would even think of me! Are we madly in love?'

Lucy flushed. 'I did imply that we were living together,' she admitted.

'Aha! Well on the way to commitment, then! Does this mean that I'll have the pleasure of your company for longer?'

'No… God, no,' she said hurriedly. 'I rang my friend Meg and I can go and stay with her tomorrow. She's out this evening, or I'd be there now.'

'You'll stay tonight, then?'

'If you don't mind,' she said a little uncomfortably, hearing the echo of his voice. There's always someone…who'll sort things out for you.

'Of course I don't mind. We're in love, aren't we?' Guy stood up and stretched. 'I'm starving. Let's go out and get something to eat.'

Lucy's stomach rumbled at the thought, but she could imagine the kind of restaurants Guy frequented. 'I'm not dressed for going out,' she said, gesturing down at herself. 'I don't have anything smarter with me.'

Guy studied her. She was wearing jeans and a camisole top, with a soft little cardigan, and the beautiful blonde hair was clipped casually up. She didn't look at all smart, it was true, but she looked fresh and natural and very pretty and, in spite of the inevitable effects of the long flight from Australia, there was a sparkle about her that no diamond necklace could have matched.

'You won't need sequins or a tiara where we're going,' he promised her. 'You look absolutely fine.'

Lucy got to her feet, still hesitating. 'To be honest with you, Guy, I haven't got much money,' she confessed at last, flushing with embarrassment. 'Meredith gave me what cash she had, but it wasn't much and I'll need to find a temporary job of some kind to see me through until I can go back to Australia. Until then, I don't think I can afford to go out.'

'Dinner's on me,' said Guy, and then, when he could see her about to protest, 'Hey, I'm your boyfriend, aren't I? I don't want you telling Richard's parents that I'm too mean to take you out!'

Overriding her feeble attempts to resist, he bore her down in the lift and out into the cold London night. Lucy had been expecting that they would go to one of the smart restaurants nearby, but instead Guy led her away from the chic shops and bars and crowds and down a maze of small streets that seemed a world away from the glittering towers of Canary Wharf.

He took her to a tiny, unpretentious Italian restaurant that Lucy would have walked past without noticing if Guy hadn't stopped and pushed open the door. Instantly they were enveloped in a fug of welcome warmth and noise. At first glance the restaurant seemed completely full, but the waiters and then the owners greeted Guy like a long-lost brother and, before they knew it, a table for two had been conjured up and was being laid with a flourish while the waiters vied to make Lucy laugh with their extravagant compliments.

'Hey, that's enough!' Guy pretended to glower at them. 'She's with me!'

After Kevin's laconic style, it was heady stuff. Kevin did strong and silent, not fun and flirtation, and, although it was just nonsense, Lucy's spirits rose in response.

Taking a sip of wine, she put down her glass and leant her elbows on the table with a happy sigh. The restaurant was throbbing with the sound of people enjoying themselves, with chatter and laughter and the warm smell of good food, while downstairs what sounded like a large party of Italians were watching football on television, their whoops and groans erupting up the stairs at regular intervals.

'This is a great place,' she told Guy, smiling. She could feel her pulse quickening and all at once she had a sense of thousands of vibrant little restaurants like this one, each full of people talking and laughing, spreading out across London. It was almost as if the city had an insistent beat to it that made her want to tap her foot.

'I'm glad you like it,' he said, his eyes on her bright face.

'It's funny to think that we were in the outback only two days ago, isn't it?' she said. 'It feels as if we've flown into a different universe. Wirrindago is so beautiful. It's so quiet and so still and so big.' She looked around the restaurant. 'All these people, all this noise…it's unimaginable there, and yet, when you're here, it's hard to imagine how isolated it is there.'

With a glance at her watch, she tried to calculate the time difference, her nose wrinkling with the effort of concentration. 'They should be having their morning smoko about now,' she worked out and the blue eyes were momentarily wistful.

'Are you missing Kevin?'

'I haven't had time to miss him yet.' Lucy picked up her wine and avoided Guy's eyes. Already Kevin seemed remote, she thought guiltily—like someone she had known in another life.

Only Guy was real. Sitting across the little table from her, he seemed extraordinarily vivid, as if everything about him was suddenly sharper and clearer in a way that left Lucy feeling uneasy. The easy pleasure she had taken in the restaurant had evaporated and in its place was a bubble of tension that cut off their table from everyone else.

'I will, though,' she told Guy, almost as if trying to convince herself. 'I'll miss him a lot.'

'Of course you will,' he agreed in a neutral voice.

Lucy was very aware of his blue eyes on her face, but she couldn't look at him. Instead she swirled the wine in her glass and watched it intently, trying not to think about the slow, disturbing thump of her heart.

She was very glad when Joe, the owner, arrived, full of smiles, to take their order. 'For you, *bella?*'

'Oh, I don't know,' said Lucy, hastily consulting the menu. 'It all looks so good…I would like everything! What can you recommend? Anything except beef!'

'For you, the special tonight…linguine with crab and just a *leetle* chilli…light, delicious, just a hint of fire…' He kissed his fingers in an extravagantly Italian gesture. 'It is beautiful, like you.'

Guy rolled his eyes at the accent and leant over confidentially. 'You know, he can speak English perfectly well, can't you, Joe? He's just showing off to impress you.'

Joe clapped his hand to his heart. 'You are just jealous because you are a buttoned-up Englishman and you do not have the words to tell Lucy how beautiful she is!'

Lucy laughed, glad at the way the strangely tense atmosphere had dissolved into humour. 'The linguine sounds fab, Joe,' she said. 'I'd like that, please.'

Joe smirked at her and turned to Guy. 'Your usual, then, is it?' he asked, switching seamlessly from a romantic Italian into a cocky Cockney, and Lucy was still bubbling with laughter as he disappeared in the direction of the kitchen.

'No need to ask if you come here often!'

'More often than I use my kitchen,' he admitted.

'You'll have to find yourself a nice girl who can cook for you,' said Lucy, lavishly buttering a piece of bread. She didn't think she could wait until her linguine was ready.

'Sadly, most of the women I know are on permanent diets,' said Guy, and she paused guiltily for a moment in mid-butter before deciding she was too hungry to care about appearances. 'They do even less cooking than I do.'

He looked across the table at Lucy, her mouth full of bread. 'I'm afraid you're the only nice girl I know who can cook.'

As their eyes met, Lucy's heart started that painful thud again, slamming slowly against her ribs in a way that made it hard to breathe. Uneasily, her gaze slid away from his and she swallowed the bread with some difficulty.

'I've already got a job at Wirrindago,' she reminded him when she could speak.

'So you do.' Guy's smile was rueful. 'I keep forgetting.'

There was a pause. Lucy pushed some breadcrumbs around her plate, unable to look at him for some reason. Her appetite had suddenly deserted her. As the silence lengthened, she pressed the crumbs on to her finger and licked them off.

'Have some more bread,' he said, offering the bread basket. His voice was very dry and, when she risked a quick glance, she found that he was watching her with an unfathomable expression.

'Thanks.' She took a piece, more for something to do with her hands than because she really wanted it. 'It was kind of you to buy me dinner,' she added stiltedly. 'I was hungry.'

'Well, you know what they say, Cinderella. There's no such thing as a free lunch—or dinner, in this case. I've got an ulterior motive.'

'Oh?' Lucy stilled, the bread halfway to her mouth, as all sorts of scenarios chased themselves through her brain, each one more unlikely than the next.

'I've got a favour to ask you.'

'Oh?' she said again weakly.

'I was wondering if you'd come and see my mother one day.'

Lucy sat up straighter. 'Your *mother*?' It was the last thing she had been expecting.

'The thing is, I think she could do with some distraction,' Guy explained. 'I know she'd like to talk to you about Wirrindago. She grew up there, and though she may have married an Englishman and made her home here, she's still an outback girl at heart, I think. She can be a bit…abrupt,' he said, choosing his words carefully, 'but she's been through some bad times, and her bark really is worse than her bite. Anyway, I'm pretty sure she would like you.' He glanced at Lucy. 'Would you mind?'

'Of course not,' she said. Given that Guy had paid for her flight, offered her a bed for the night and was buying her this dinner, it seemed the least she could do. And it was such a relief to feel that awful tension dissipate again that she would have agreed to anything. 'I'd like to meet her.'

'Really? That's great.' Guy seemed genuinely relieved. 'Perhaps we could arrange something when she's home after the operation?'

'I'm sure that would be fine. I'll give you my mobile number and you can call me or text me.'

'Ma will be delighted,' he said, pouring Lucy some more wine. 'I think part of her problem at the moment is that she's bored. She's always been so active, but her arthritis has meant that she hasn't been able to get out much recently. All she's had to do is sit at home and complain about me. There's lots of scope there, of course, but even she gets tired of going over the same old ground after a while.'

'Gosh, what does she criticise you about?'

Guy leant back in his chair and grinned. 'Well, that depends on her mood. My wasted youth is a favourite, or it can be something I'm wearing that she doesn't approve of. If I turn up in a pink shirt, that's it for the evening! At the moment it's my failure to get married, settle down and provide her with grandchildren that is her biggest gripe.' He made a face, but Lucy didn't think that he seemed particularly crushed. 'I split up with my girlfriend before I left for Australia, so it's a sore subject.'

Ah. Lucy had been wondering why there was no sign of a girlfriend and, since he had raised the subject, she didn't see why she shouldn't be nosy and ask about it.

'What happened?'

'Nothing dramatic,' said Guy. 'There was just no chemistry for either of us…and I do think a relationship needs some flash and dazzle, don't you?' he said, eyes gleaming, and Lucy had the nasty feeling that he was thinking of her relationship with Kevin.

There hadn't been a chance for any flash and dazzle with Kevin, she thought, but she didn't see why she should tell Guy that. Let him think that she and Kevin had barely had to touch each other for the sparks to be flying—as they *would* have done if they had ever managed to snatch more than a few moments alone, Lucy reassured herself.

'Yes, I do,' she said and met his eyes squarely. No way was she going to let Guy suspect she was at all flustered by talking about sex with him. 'I think physical attraction is a hugely important part of a relationship.'

'Well, that's what was lacking with Anna and me. It's not that she isn't attractive—she is—but we didn't make each other's heart beat faster.'

Uncomfortably aware that her own heart was beating rather faster than normal, Lucy reached for more bread and wished Joe would hurry up with her linguine.

'So it was a mutual decision?'

'Yes, but you'd never hear my mother accepting that,' said Guy. 'She didn't like my previous girlfriend—she said she was too thin—and when Cassie went back to her old boyfriend, she was heartily relieved. Then I met Anna, and Ma thought she was great. She's convinced Anna left me because I didn't ask her to marry me quickly enough, and now she's blaming everything that goes wrong—including her hip operation—on what she calls my "morbid fear of commit-ment"!'

His tone was light, but Lucy wondered if he cared more than he was prepared to admit.

'*Are* you afraid of commitment?' she asked.

'No,' said Guy. 'I'm thirty-three and I've got to the stage where I wouldn't mind finding the girl I want to spend the rest of my life with, but I'm not going to let my mother push me into marriage just because she wants grandchildren. I've told her that I'll get married when I've found the right girl.'

'And you haven't found her yet?'

Blue eyes looked into blue. 'No,' he said slowly, almost as if he wasn't quite sure. 'Not yet.'

CHAPTER FOUR

THERE was another of those silences when all the air seemed to leak out of Lucy's lungs and she could feel herself prickling with awareness. She was intensely glad when Joe reappeared beside them, bearing two steaming plates.

'*Buon appetito!*' he said at his most Italian, and waved over a waiter. By the time they'd finished with the pepper and the Parmesan and the topping up of the glasses, the awkward moment had passed.

The linguine was as delicious as Joe had promised, but it was hard to eat gracefully. 'It's lucky we're not on a date,' Lucy said indistinctly as she sucked in a loose strand of pasta.

'Oh, I don't know,' said Guy, amused. 'If I were your boyfriend—or hoping to be—I would like the way you eat. You do it the way you do everything else, with gusto.'

'Meredith says I've got too much enthusiasm.' Inexpertly, Lucy twirled another mouthful of pasta around her fork. 'She says I should learn to think before I act.'

He looked interested. 'Do you think that's true?'

'Well…sometimes I get into situations and find that they're not quite what I imagined,' she admitted, 'but things usually work out—and it's not always because Meredith rescues me,' she added before he could suggest it.

'What sort of situations?' he asked, intrigued.

Meredith would say that she fell in and out of love too easily, Lucy knew, and maybe in the past there *had* been one or two occasions when her infatuation had burned itself out pretty quickly...but of course all that had changed now that she had met Kevin.

'Romantic situations occasionally,' she admitted cagily, 'but also with jobs. I don't have the most impressive CV in the world.'

'Is that a way of saying that you've started a lot of jobs and never stuck with any of them?'

She eyed him with a touch of resentment. 'Sometimes you sound annoyingly like Meredith,' she informed him. 'I prefer to think of it as having wide experience,' she went on. 'I've been a waitress, a secretary, a cook... What else? Oh, yes, I've done a stint in PR for a charity, I worked in a call centre—that was *awful*—and a shop, which was quite fun. I was a tourist guide once and I even sold houses for a bit before I went to Australia, although I wasn't very good at that.'

'You're obviously not lacking in ability,' said Guy. 'Have you ever thought about a real job?'

'The depends on what you mean by a real job,' said Lucy, slightly on the defensive as always when it came to her career, or lack of one.

'A job that really stretches and stimulates you,' he said. 'A job that allows you to reach your full potential. That's what I call a real job.'

'What, like working in a family bank? How stretching can that be?'

'You'd be surprised.' Guy was unfazed by her sarcasm. 'I spent most of my twenties messing around like you. It wasn't easy to settle down and learn to take work seriously, but I've learnt a lot.'

'We don't all want to be tied down to nine to five. Some of us are free spirits,' she said grandly. 'I deliberately choose short-term jobs that mean I can go where I want, when I want. It's called being independent.'

'Or is it called always taking the easy option? After all, nobody expects a temp to tackle anything very difficult, do they?'

Lucy's blue eyes narrowed dangerously. 'Are you suggesting that I'm lazy?'

'Are you?'

'No, and I resent the implication that I am! I worked really hard at Wirrindago.'

'That's true,' he conceded. 'But it wasn't difficult. You didn't try and do anything that you hadn't done before. You're a good cook, but turning out roast dinners and cakes isn't exactly a challenge for you, is it? I doubt if you learnt anything more about yourself and what you're capable of at Wirrindago,' he said.

Lucy hunched a shoulder. 'Why would I need to learn *about* myself? I know who I am.'

'Do you?' Guy didn't bother to hide his scepticism. 'You were very quick to issue challenges at the rodeo, Cinders, but have you ever thought about challenging yourself?'

'Oh, *please!*' She rolled her eyes extravagantly. 'You sound like Meredith!'

He pointed his fork at her. 'Or is the truth that you avoid challenging situations because you're scared?'

'What have I got to be scared about?'

'You might be scared in case all this being a free spirit and choosing to be independent is really about running away from responsibility, about being afraid in case you can't do anything more than mess around.'

'That's rubbish!' said Lucy furiously. 'I'm not scared of anything!'

Guy studied her face for a moment, and then he put down his fork with a faint smile as he leant across the table towards her.

'Prove it,' he said.

Prove it. Lucy stared back at him, hearing the echo of her own words at the rodeo. Prove it, she had said to him as they'd stood by that fence, surrounded by the heat and the noise and the smell of dust and horses, and he had.

'I can't just embark on a career just to prove to you that I'm not scared of responsibility,' she said. 'I'm going back to Australia as soon as I can, so the only job I can commit to is a temporary one. And I won't need a fancy CV to get one either,' she added, stung by his lack of belief in her. 'I can get a job wherever and *when*ever I want,' she declared and snapped her fingers between them. 'Just like that!'

'OK, then, let's make it a different challenge.' Guy rubbed his jaw thoughtfully. 'Let's see, it's Thursday today. If you put your mind to it, you could get yourself a job tomorrow and start work on Monday.

'And I don't mean asking any of your friends to find you something,' he warned as Lucy opened her mouth. 'You have to do it on your own, and try something you've never done before, in a reputable organisation. No wacky outfits or off-beat cafés. I want you to prove to me that you can get a job and take it seriously.'

'Even if it's just a temporary job?'

'Yes. How long do you think you'll be here—a month? That's long enough to prove that you're not afraid to push yourself a bit harder.'

Lucy bit her lip. 'You know, it would be a lot easier if you'd just take my word for it,' she quoted, and Guy smiled, recognising his own words.

'But then it wouldn't be a challenge, would it, Cinders?' The blue gaze held hers. 'Well? Are you going to stick with what you know, or are you going to show me what you're made of?'

'I'll do it if you promise never to call me Cinders again,' she said grouchily.

Guy clicked his tongue in mock gentle reproof. 'I'm the one setting the terms of the challenge here. You've had your go, and I don't remember me being given any option to negotiate!'

'Oh, very well.' Lucy lifted her chin. 'I'll take your challenge. I need to get myself a job anyway, to keep me going until I know what's happening with Richard. I can do that by Monday.' Draining her glass, she met his eyes squarely. 'You're on!'

It had felt good to accept Guy's challenge, but how exactly was she going to do it? Lucy wondered as they walked back to his apartment, having taken an extravagant farewell of Joe, the waiters and even the football fans who had come up after the match to enjoy a boisterous meal on the next table.

In spite of her confidence, she knew that serious jobs, even temporary ones, weren't that easy to come by when all you really had going for you was charm of manner. She would find something though, Lucy vowed. Guy clearly thought that she was feckless, silly, lazy and spoilt—which was pretty good coming from someone who had apparently walked into a job in the family firm and didn't appear to take anything seriously! Not everyone was lucky enough to have a handy bank in the family when it came to getting a job.

Well, she would show him. Lucy's mouth set in a stubborn line. She would get herself a job at Dangerfield & Dunn itself. That ought to be a reputable enough organisation for him. The name of the family bank was emblazoned on message pads and stray pens and cards around Guy's flat. It would be no problem to find their address on the Internet, and then all she would need to do was persuade someone there to give her a job.

Starting Monday.

Mentally, Lucy waved that aside as a minor detail to be dealt with at a later stage. *Somehow* she would get herself a job at Dangerfield & Dunn, she promised herself, and not only that, she would be the best employee they had ever had. Guy would be down on his knees begging her to stay before she left.

They were walking along the old quays of London's docks, lined now with aggressively modern apartment blocks. The Thames gleamed dully, and the ghosts of the great ships that had once been tied to the massive bollards that were all that survived of those times seemed to shimmer in the fuzzy yellow light that was the closest London ever got to darkness.

Lucy shivered and pulled her jacket closer around her.

'Cold?'

'It's not the outback, is it?' she said by way of a reply. Pausing by one of the bollards, she looked out over the river. 'At Wirrindago, the stars are incredible. So many of them, and so clear…' She sighed a little, remembering. 'You can't see the stars at all here.'

'It doesn't mean they're not there,' said Guy. 'But you're right, a London night always seems a bit murky in comparison to Wirrindago. It's a special place,' he said, his voice warm with affection. 'I do understand why you love it so much. I do, too.'

'But you can go whenever you want,' she pointed out. 'Your mother's Australian, so presumably you wouldn't have any problem getting a visa,' she added enviously. 'You could live there if you wanted to.'

'I could, but my life is here,' he said. 'My home, my work, friends, my mother…and, of course, my new girlfriend.'

New girlfriend? Lucy was alarmed by the way her heart plummeted at the thought. 'I didn't know you had a new girl-friend,' she said as casually as she could.

'Oh, yes, she's very pretty.' His smile gleamed in the darkness. 'A little contrary at times, but she's got the bluest blue eyes full of sunshine, and her hair is beautiful.'

Reaching out, he wound a stray tendril of Lucy's hair around his finger, and she couldn't prevent a treacherous shiver at the warm brush of his hand against her neck. 'Some people might say it was blonde,' he went on, his voice deep and rippling with laughter, 'but it's much more than that. It's shot through with silver and spun gold, with amber and honey and sunlight, and it looks so silky that all you want to do is let it down and tangle your fingers in it.'

Half mesmerised by his voice and his smile and his near-ness, it took Lucy a moment to realise that she could step back quite easily. 'I'm not your girlfriend,' she said, appalled at how breathless she sounded.

'Well, that's not what you were telling Richard's parents earlier this evening!' Guy clutched at his heart, pretending that he was wounded, and Lucy sucked in her breath, torn between intense irritation and a rather alarming desire to laugh.

'You know perfectly well that I didn't mean you,' she told him, turning to walk once more. 'I told them my boyfriend was called Guy, but that's all you've got in common. He's nothing like you!'

'That's a shame.' Guy fell into step beside her. 'So what's he like, then?'

'My boyfriend, Guy? Well, let's see.' Lucy tilted her head and considered. Why should Guy have all the fun? 'He's utterly gorgeous, of course.'

'*Is* he?'

'He's kind and sweet and chivalrous, and he absolutely

adores me. He's always bringing me little presents, and telling me how much he loves me.'

'He sounds a bit sickly to me.' Guy made a face.

'He's not sickly. He's lovely,' said Lucy firmly.

'I suppose he's a real man, too?'

'Naturally. He's steady and intelligent and very responsible. He never makes stupid jokes or gives people silly nicknames.'

Guy sighed and took her hand to tuck it into the crook of his arm. 'I don't think he's the man for you, Cinders.'

'He's perfect for me.'

'Perfect is dull,' he told her. '*I* think you need someone who's a bit more fun. Someone who doesn't always play by the rules.'

'What rules?'

'The rules that say you don't kiss a girl when you know she's in love with someone else,' said Guy, stopping so that Lucy, her hand still in his arm, ended up stopping too and, before she had realised quite what was happening, he had pulled her round to face him.

With his free hand, he reached up and pulled the clip from her hair so that it tumbled down to her shoulders. 'The rules that say you should just take her home and say goodnight,' he said softly. 'The rules that say you shouldn't keep her standing out in the cold and the dark so that you can do this…'

Everything seemed to be happening in slow motion. Every sense in Lucy's body seemed to be quivering, although whether with alarm or anticipation she couldn't quite be sure. Certainly when Guy's mouth came down on hers the earth seemed to tilt and her heart gave a great jolt that could only be shock, but instead of pulling away, as she knew that she could have done, some different message was parting her lips, was thrilling to the taste of his mouth and urging her to lean into the warmth and sureness of his touch.

She could move away, Lucy knew. She could stop this, and really she ought to do it, she ought to do it *now*, in fact, but kissing him felt so *right* somehow. It was almost as if there were something inevitable about finding herself in his arms, something that left her in thrall to the feel of his lips, to the tantalising exploration of his tongue, to the shudder of desire that ran through her when he pulled her closer, one hand caressing her spine, the other possessively curved beneath her hair at the nape of her neck, his palm warm against the sensitive skin as the kiss deepened.

Lucy was twenty-six and without any vanity had always known herself to be a pretty girl. She had been kissed lots of times before, but never—*never*—like this. Never before had she felt her bones dissolve beneath the upsurge of honeyed pleasure. Never had she felt this deep, dark, delicious thrum of possession and *power*. Her fingers might clutch his jacket, but she wasn't a weak, helpless thing. She was an equal in passion, an equal in the kiss, an equal in the slow burn of need.

The kissing was lovely, but it wasn't enough. Inside her, the excitement was rapidly uncoiling, whipping round and round until Lucy had lost control and was so tangled in it that she didn't know where she was or what she was doing. She just knew that she wanted more…

And that was when Guy slowly, reluctantly, lifted his head. For a long moment, he just looked down into her face with a twisted smile. 'I'm sorry,' he said. 'I shouldn't have done that. I just couldn't resist.'

His words reached Lucy through such a fog of confusion and churning emotions that none of them made sense.

'Wh-what was that for?' she stammered.

'What is any kiss for?' said Guy lightly, and then frowned

at the dazed expression in her eyes. 'Are you all right?' he asked, touching her cheek lightly with his fingers.

No, Lucy wanted to shout. *I'm not all right!* She was shaken and confused by the abrupt return to reality, shocked by the strength of her own reaction to his kiss and appalled by the impulse to throw herself back into his arms.

Horrified by how easily she had succumbed to his kiss.

She hadn't even made a token protest, Lucy realised, burning with humiliation.

'I'm fine.' With an enormous effort, she pulled herself together. 'Absolutely fine.'

'Are you sure?' asked Guy in concern. 'You look as if you've been knocked for six.'

Lucy wasn't up in cricketing metaphors, but she felt as if she had been knocked for a lot more than six. She wasn't ready to admit to that, though, least of all to Guy.

'I've been kissed before,' she snapped, terrified in case he guessed how much that kiss had affected her.

'I don't doubt that for a minute,' said Guy, and Lucy eyed him suspiciously.

'It's not a big deal,' she insisted.

'Good,' he said, 'because I really am sorry. I shouldn't have kissed you just now.'

Putting his hand under her elbow, he turned and started walking as if nothing whatsoever had happened. 'Usually I do stick to the rules,' he said wryly. 'I blame that boyfriend you invented. He's clearly the kind of man who takes liberties!'

'I hope he's not expecting to take any more tonight,' said Lucy, who had recovered somewhat, although she was still a lot more shaken than she wanted to admit.

'Absolutely not,' said Guy. 'Scout's honour, in fact.' Solemnly, he held up crossed fingers, only to spoil the effect by adding, 'It *was* only a kiss, after all.'

Right. Just a kiss.

She had told Guy that it wasn't a big deal and it wasn't, Lucy told herself repeatedly that night. Jetlag was the only reason she couldn't get to sleep. Obviously.

Lucy sighed and turned over and thumped her pillow but she couldn't get comfortable. She was buzzing with the memory of the way he had kissed her, and just when she thought she had pushed it firmly into a box at the back of her mind marked *No Big Deal*, it would come bursting out again in heart-shaking detail.

The touch of his lips, the taste of his mouth, the feel of his hard hands… Worse, her own eagerness, the shameful ease with which she had been seduced by sensation and abandoned herself to pleasure. How she had clutched at him, how her tongue had teased his, how she had returned kiss for kiss as if they were lovers.

'Aaargh…' Lucy groaned and buried her face in the pillow. How *could* she? She had had plenty of opportunity to push Guy scornfully away, so why hadn't she done it? She didn't even *like* him! Well, not much, anyway. She was in love with Kevin, who would never have kissed her like that—if only he had!—and you didn't kiss other men when you felt like that, no matter how little a deal it was.

Sighing, she threw herself over on to her back once more and stared resentfully at the ceiling. What a great evening! She had been accused of laziness and cowardice, and then humiliated with a stupid kiss. Well, she would show Guy that it took more than that to get her down! Tomorrow, she was going out to get herself a job, and they would see who was humiliated then.

Lucy paused outside Dangerfield & Dunn and looked up at the striking soaring façade, the glass reflecting the blue of a spring sky. It was nothing like her idea of an investment bank.

Instead it was all sleek design and cutting-edge technology and the unmistakable hush of serious money.

She could hardly believe that she had blagged her way into a job in such a place, but even investment banks oozing wealth and power were not immune from day-to-day hassles. One of the receptionists, an actress who had suddenly been offered a part, had left without warning that Friday, and when Lucy had called in to see if she could wheedle her way into an interview with Human Resources the surviving receptionist had been struggling to deal with a queue of people wanting information while the phones buzzed frantically.

Seeing that she was overwhelmed, Lucy had walked round and started answering the phone. It was a simple matter to explain that the receptionist was unavailable and to offer to take a message, and it was surprising how many people simply said that they would call back later.

Imogen, the harried receptionist, had looked at her gratefully when the rush was past.

'What were you doing here?' she asked when she had thanked her.

'I'm looking for a temporary job.'

Imogen smiled. 'You've got it. When can you start?'

So here Lucy was on Monday morning. Tugging down the jacket of the suit she had borrowed from Meg, she mentally squared her shoulders. Around her streamed smartly dressed men and women, all hurrying past with purposeful strides, and in spite of herself she was caught up in the buzz of the City. Maybe this job wouldn't be so bad.

Granted, she was no high-powered executive with millions to play with before lunch, and receptionist might not have been her first choice of career, but it was perfect for now. Guy would have to walk past her every day, and Lucy couldn't wait to see his face when he saw her sitting behind the reception desk.

He had been long gone by the time she'd woken the morning after their visit to Giovanni's. Lucy had been relieved that she didn't have to face him while the memory of that shattering kiss was still tingling along her veins, but there was a bit of her that was a little miffed that he hadn't bothered to say goodbye before she moved out to stay with Meg.

She had left her mobile phone number with a scribbled note of thanks. It didn't seem that she could go without a word, even if it hadn't bothered Guy to do just that. Besides, how else could he get in touch with her about his mother? Lucy had told herself that was all she was thinking about when she'd written the note. It had nothing whatsoever to do with making sure that he had no excuse not to contact her.

Imogen was waiting to greet her in the dramatic atrium with a roof that soared upwards past a mezzanine floor. The reception desk was strikingly shaped and set near the glass-sided lifts. It bristled with the latest technology that Lucy eyed askance at first but, once Imogen had showed her how to use it, it didn't seem quite so intimidating and she thought she might be able to manage it after all.

Lucy was kept busy dealing with a steady stream of visitors and phone calls while Imogen, who seemed to be an authority on Dangerfield & Dunn, filled her in on the background to the bank. The name that cropped up most often was Guy's.

'He's just a figurehead, right?' Lucy asked at last, and Imogen looked shocked.

'He's Chairman and Chief Executive.'

'Well, yes, but it's a family bank, isn't it? Presumably he only gets to be Chairman because he's a Dangerfield. Who does all the real work?'

'He does,' said Imogen reprovingly. 'Guy's the one who makes the decisions. I think it's been a bit of a battle in the boardroom since his father died,' she confided, 'but he's turning things round and Dangerfield & Dunn are now the leaders in ethical investment. He's only thirty-three, but Guy Dangerfield is already a name to be reckoned with in the financial world,' she finished proudly.

It was soon obvious that Imogen was Guy's biggest fan. 'He's lovely to work for, and so thoughtful! I've got a friend in marketing who'd been working for ages on a Open University degree, and when she passed Guy sent her flowers and a bottle of champagne.'

'It sounds to me as if he's got a thoughtful PA,' said Lucy, unimpressed, but Imogen leapt instantly to his defence.

'It was Guy's idea,' she insisted. 'And when he found out one of the other girls had been going through a bad time at home, he told her to take the day off and sent her a voucher for a day at a spa!'

Imogen sighed. 'He's so gorgeous, too. Well, you must have seen him. It's enough to make a girl wish she wasn't happily married,' she went on without waiting for Lucy's answer. 'Not that he'd look at me even if I wasn't,' she said honestly. 'He always has incredibly glamorous girlfriends.'

'You're glamorous,' said Lucy, and told herself that she didn't care in the least that Guy had a taste for glamour and sophistication as opposed to, say, a free spirit in jeans and a T-shirt. Imogen was just confirming what she had already guessed from Guy's apartment.

'Not like Cassandra Wolfe,' said Imogen, but she looked pleased nonetheless.

'Who?'

'You know! The supermodel!'

'Oh…yes.' Lucy had never been particularly interested in gossip columns but even she had heard of Cassandra Wolfe, one of the few celebrities who could be referred to simply by her first name.

So she was presumably the Cassie Guy had mentioned so casually at Giovanni's. Remembering what she had seen of Cassandra Wolfe, Lucy wasn't at all surprised Guy's mother had thought she was too thin.

Imogen, it seemed, was an endless source of information about Guy. 'She and Guy split up a couple of months ago and now Cassandra's back with her ex-boyfriend.'

'The rock singer?' It was all coming back to Lucy now. There had been some big scandal before she'd left for Australia.

Imogen nodded. 'I'd have stuck with Guy if it was me,' she said.

'So was Guy very upset when she left him?' Lucy couldn't help asking.

'Not so as you could tell,' Imogen admitted. 'He always seems in a good humour when I see him, and he's got a lovely smile.'

Lucy knew the smile she meant.

'He went out with some titled girl after Cassandra, but we never saw her here,' Imogen went on. 'I haven't heard of her for a while, but Guy's been away in Australia.' Her eyes brightened. 'Maybe he's on the market again. I hope so.'

Lucy fixed her with a mock severe look. 'I thought you were happily married?'

'I am.' Imogen grinned. 'But you're not, are you? You could be in with a chance!'

'With Guy Dangerfield? I don't think so. He's not my type,' said Lucy casually, in spite of some very uncomfortable memories jumping up and down and insisting that he had been *exactly* her type when he'd kissed her. 'He's a bit obvious for me.'

Imogen looked at her as if she were mad, but Lucy rushed to change the subject. She couldn't help thinking that they had talked about Guy quite enough. Anyone would think that she was interested in him.

There was no sign of him coming in to work and, having looked forward to his expression when he saw that she had met her challenge, Lucy was vaguely disgruntled at the fact that he hadn't bothered to come in. He was probably playing golf or squash, she decided with an inward sniff. Perhaps he would swan in later when the lifts weren't so busy and he wouldn't have to mingle with the workers.

She could picture the scene perfectly. A limousine like the one that had met them at Heathrow would pull up outside and out would step Guy, ready for a couple of hours of being toadied to by the likes of Imogen before it was time to go home.

Lucy's lips pursed at the thought. No, she for one wouldn't be rushing to bow and scrape when he arrived. Yes, Guy was generous, she'd give him that, but as he himself had pointed out, he could afford it. And generosity didn't stop him being deeply irritating, and the kind of man who would kiss you till your bones melted and then tell you it was only a kiss.

And then leave the next morning without even bothering to say goodbye.

'Here he is!' Imogen hissed, sitting up straighter. Lucy was looking at the doors where a limousine had drawn up, but there was no sign of Guy yet.

'Where—?' she began, turning to Imogen and following her gaze to the bank of lifts, where three men had evidently just stepped out.

Guy was talking and the two others were listening deferentially. All three were immaculately dressed in suits, but somehow Lucy saw only Guy. He had his back to her and her heart jerked in instant recognition of the set of his shoulders, of the back of his head and the air of suppressed energy he exuded. There was a kind of coiled power in the easy way he held himself and at the sight of him Lucy felt as if a great fist were clenching and unclenching deep inside her.

They were all shaking hands now and his two companions disappeared back into the lifts while Guy headed for the car waiting outside in blatant disregard of the double yellow lines.

'Morning, Imogen!' he called as he walked past.

'Morning!' Imogen simpered.

Evidently registering that there was someone else sitting beside her, Guy's smile swept on, only to freeze as he did a satisfactory double take at the sight of Lucy, demure in the little checked suit that she had borrowed from Meg.

'Lucy?' he said, stopping dead, and Lucy felt Imogen turn to stare at her.

Savouring the astonishment in his expression, Lucy smiled graciously. 'Good morning, Mr Dangerfield,' she said sweetly.

Recovering swiftly, he came over to the desk. 'It's Guy,' he corrected her. 'We're all on first-name terms here, aren't we, Imogen?'

Imogen nodded eagerly.

'Well, well, well, as the three oilmen said.' Guy's smile broadened as he turned to study Lucy, who was rolling her eyes at Imogen's worshipful expression.

Meg's suit didn't sit entirely easily on her, but she had obviously made a great effort to conform. The beautiful hair that was usually carelessly gathered up into a clip and allowed to fall any old how had been neatly braided into a French plait, and she was discreetly made-up, her blue eyes emphasised with mascara—also borrowed from Meg, had he but known it—and lipstick on the generous curving mouth. She looked older and more sophisticated, but her expression was as bright as ever.

'Congratulations,' he said. 'You've surprised me, Cinders. I have to admit that I didn't expect you to have a job by this morning, let alone here. Why did no one tell me that you'd be working here?'

'I'm sure you're much too busy to be bothered with trivial details like the temporary receptionist,' said Lucy, studiedly cool, which was hard when his eyes were on her face and the glinting smile in the blue depths was as unsettling as ever.

'I'm never too busy to be interested in my staff, Lucy.'

'That's just what I've been telling her,' Imogen put in loyally, and Guy smiled at her.

'As you've obviously gathered, Lucy and I have met before,' he said.

'In Australia,' Lucy put in quickly before he could say any more. 'But we don't really know each other well, do we, Guy? Things are different now that we're back in London.'

'They are, indeed,' said Guy, and somehow she knew that he was thinking about how they had kissed on the quayside. 'Very different.'

CHAPTER FIVE

GUY was on his way out to a meeting, he said, so couldn't stay. 'But I'll look forward to catching up with you later, Lucy. It's going to be interesting having you here!'

Waving a farewell, he headed out through the doors, while Lucy was careful not to look at Imogen.

'Is there anything I should know?' asked Imogen pointedly when the waiting limousine had pulled away.

'No. Honestly,' she insisted when Imogen looked sceptical. 'He was a guest at the cattle station where I was working and we happened to come back to London on the same flight. That's all. We barely know each other.'

Which in one sense was quite true. She *didn't* know Guy. She didn't know what went on behind that façade of lazy good humour. She didn't know what made him tick, what he thought and hoped and dreamed. All she knew about him was the smile in his eyes, the sureness of his throw, the easy way he could swing into the saddle.

And the way he kissed. She knew the taste of his lips and the touch of his hands, the dizzy delight of pressing in to him and kissing him back.

'We're acquaintances, at the most.'

Guy came back about three—obviously a long lunch, Lucy

sniffed to herself—but although he lifted a hand in greeting as he made his way to the lifts, he didn't come over to speak to them. Why should he, after all? She was just a reception-ist in a borrowed suit. Lucy told herself that she didn't care, and that she hoped he would stay up in his penthouse office from now on. She had met his challenge, and now it would be much easier if she had nothing more to do with him.

If Guy wanted her, he knew where to find her. She wasn't going to start looking for *him*.

But it was hard not to look up every time the lift doors slid open, hard to stop the tiny treacherous dip of her heart every time it wasn't him.

By the end of the day, Lucy was exhausted with the effort of concentrating on all the new information, and she was glad when Imogen announced that they could both go home. She wasn't looking forward to the journey back to Meg's, though. The unfamiliar shoes had been pinching all day and it was a long walk back from the tube.

Imogen had buttoned herself into her coat and was hurry-ing off to meet her husband. Lucy waved goodbye and col-lected her things, moving very gingerly on her sore feet, and joined the exodus. People were spilling out of the lifts and streaming towards the exit, all as anxious to get home as she was, but moving rather more swiftly. Lucy had just reached the doors when a familiar voice spoke in her ear.

'You know, I don't think I've ever seen your legs before,' said Guy, as if it were perfectly normal to start in mid-conversation. 'It's a shame to keep them hidden behind that reception desk, especially when you're wearing such spec-tacular shoes.'

Lucy followed his gaze down to Meg's shoes which were, indeed, spectacular. They were made of turquoise suede, with cutaway sides and vertiginous heels. Lucy had loved the look of them, and Meg was right, they did go brilliantly with the suit, but she was feeling a lot less enamoured after wearing them all day.

'I borrowed them from the friend I'm staying with,' she told Guy, rather pleased at how normal she sounded given that her heart was performing an elaborate tap dance routine against her ribs. 'Fortunately, we're the same size. Meg loves high heels, but I'm not used to walking in them yet.'

'I can see that you'd need a good sense of balance,' commented Guy. 'I hope you haven't got far to walk.'

'Miles.' Lucy sighed without thinking.

'Come on, I'll give you a lift,' he said, taking her by the arm. 'The car's just outside.'

'Oh, really, it's not—'

Ignoring her feeble attempts at protest, and the curious looks of those who were clearly wondering what the Chief Executive was doing with the new receptionist, Guy propelled her out of the door.

'You don't really want to wait ages for a bus or to battle with the tube on those shoes, do you?'

No, she really didn't, Lucy had to admit. It seemed easier just to give in and climb into the back of the limousine. She couldn't help a sigh of relief as she sank back into the luxurious leather and eased off the shoes. She wasn't sure that she would ever be able to get them on again, but, right then, Lucy didn't care.

'Where are you staying?' Guy asked as he climbed in beside her and the car pulled away from the kerb.

'Bethnal Green,' Lucy told him, 'but actually I'm on my way to see Richard now,' she added quickly, seeing him lean forward to talk to the chauffeur. 'If you could drop me near the hospital, that would be great.'

Guy murmured the change of instruction to the driver and

then sat back beside her. Immediately it felt as if the space inside the car had shrunk. Lucy could feel a fluttering deep
inside her and she made herself take a steadying breath. She
had sat beside him all the way back from Australia, and on
the long drive back to Wirrindago after the rodeo. It was
stupid to be so aware of him now, on a ten-minute trip across
London.

Still, she found herself wishing that she was wearing jeans
after all. Meg had a penchant for short skirts and, even though
Guy was politely not staring at them, Lucy was very conscious of her exposed legs. Surreptitiously, she tried to tug the
skirt down a bit further towards her knees.

'I heard how you got the job,' said Guy. 'I'm impressed.'

'I told you I could get a job by Monday.' Lucy put up her
chin. 'I hope you think Dangerfield & Dunn count as a "reputable organisation"?'

'Oh, yes, I'm quite prepared to admit that you met the first
part of the challenge.'

'The *first* part?'

'You've got to push yourself, Cinders. You've done well
to get the job, but now I want to see if you can make something of it.'

'There's a limit to what you can achieve as a receptionist,'
grumbled Lucy, but he only tutted.

'That's the wrong attitude. Let's just see what you can do.'

Lucy sighed and looked out of the window. The glass was
darkened so that they could see the commuters hurrying along
the pavements, but no one could see in. It was like being in
their own quiet, dim world, cut off from the noise and the
hassle of city life.

'So where have you been all weekend?' asked Guy after a
moment. 'I missed you when I got back to the flat on Friday
and you were gone!'

'I went to stay with my friend, Meg,' said Lucy, not averse to moving the conversation away from the challenges she still apparently had to meet. 'She's got a tiny spare room which she said I could have for a couple of months. It's not much more than a cupboard, but I don't have a lot of stuff so it's fine for me, and I certainly couldn't afford to pay proper rent.'

'Is Meg an old friend?'

She nodded. 'We were at school together. She's got some hot-shot job in a law firm now and she's got loads of suits and shoes that I can wear, which is lucky because I've got no money until pay day.'

'I'm sure it would be possible to arrange an advance if you need it,' said Guy in a neutral voice.

'Oh, I'll be fine. Meg has said she'll lend me some cash if I need it.'

Or did that just mean she was letting Meg look after her the way Meredith usually did?

Lucy shook the uncomfortable thought aside.

'Meg's good fun. There aren't usually any other women at Wirrindago, and I hadn't realised how much I'd missed sitting down for a good gossip.'

'Enough to make you change your mind about going back?'

'No.' She ruffled up immediately. Why was Guy so determined to believe that her feelings for Kevin weren't real?

Of course, the fact that she had kissed him back the other night might have made him wonder if she was quite as besotted as she claimed to be, but he would have to be incredibly conceited to think that it had made a difference to her.

He *was* incredibly conceited, of course, so maybe that was exactly what he thought. She had told him that the kiss hadn't bothered her. It had, but Guy wasn't to know that.

Her chin lifted. 'Of course I'm going back,' she said. 'That doesn't mean I can't make the most of being here.'

'I'd be disappointed if you didn't, Cinders,' said Guy. 'Making the most of the moment is what you do best.'

Why was it that conversations with Guy always ended up wandering into uncomfortable territory? Lucy wondered. She never knew quite how to take comments like that.

'There's better news about Richard,' she offered in an attempt to change the subject—again! 'I've been going to the hospital every day and he's out of his coma.'

'So Meredith was right after all,' he said. 'Your voice did make the difference.'

'We can't know that.' Lucy shifted uncomfortably. She didn't like to think of Richard loving her as much as Meredith and his parents seemed to think, because that would mean she would have to hurt him again one day. 'I'm sure it's just co-incidence,' she said. 'He's still very ill and can't talk much, but obviously it's progress.'

'Well, that's good news. His parents must be relieved.'

'They're delighted, of course…'

'But?'

She made a face. 'It's very difficult. They're treating me like a daughter-in-law already. I don't know if it's just that they don't really listen when I mention my boyfriend, or if they don't believe me, but it's getting really embarrassing.'

'You can't have been talking about me enough.'

Guy's voice was threaded with amusement and Lucy cursed the moment she had told Richard's parents that her invented boyfriend was called Guy. Why on earth hadn't she chosen Paul or Jack or…Ethelbald? Anything other than Guy!

'I don't talk about you at all,' she said with a quelling look. 'I *do* try and mention my fictional lover as much as I can, but it doesn't seem to have much effect. I can't keep going on about him. I'm already pretending that he's completely besotted with me. If I'm not careful, I'll end up marrying myself to him!'

'I'm sure Guy won't mind,' said Guy. 'He'll have been a lost man as soon as he kissed you.'

A tide of colour flooded Lucy's cheeks and she was desperately grateful for the dim light in the back of the car. Beside her, Guy seemed very big and very close and her whole body was thumping with awareness of him as the air between them thrummed with the memory of that kiss on the quayside. She was sure that he must be able to hear her heart thudding.

'It was stupid to have started the whole story,' she muttered, turning to stare out of the window and willing her flush to fade. 'I shouldn't have said anything.'

'Well, it's done now,' said Guy practically. 'You could tell Richard's parents that you made the whole thing up, but that would probably be embarrassing for them, as well as for you.'

'I know. I've thought of that, but they've got enough to cope with at the moment.' She sighed. 'I'm just going to have to learn to think before I open my big mouth.'

The rush hour traffic was moving slowly and the car edged to a halt in front of yet another red light. Lucy glanced at her watch. Her feet might appreciate the ride, but it might have been quicker—and less unsettling—to have stuck with the tube.

'Do you ever think of using public transport?'

'As it happens, I do if I'm just going home, but I've got a few things on tonight. I'm going to see my mother in the hospital, and then there's a reception at the Guildhall, and later I'm going out to dinner with friends in Putney, so it just seemed easier to take the car and let Steve earn some overtime. It's one of the benefits of being a bloated plutocrat!'

'How did your mother's operation go?'

'Pretty well, the doctors think. They're making her walk already. She had a double hip replacement so it was quite a big operation, but, as far as I can tell, she's assumed command of the whole ward and the medical staff are clearly longing for the time when she's ready to go home!'

'When will that be?' asked Lucy.

'Next week some time, I think. The occupational therapist has been to Ma's house and I've had a list of things to organise to make things easier for when she comes out of hospital. I've had a second banister fitted to the stairs and bought her a new armchair and a higher bed, but I'm braced to discover that I've chosen absolutely the wrong thing.'

His voice was light, but Lucy didn't laugh. She glanced at him, a tiny crease between her eyes.

'I would have thought that someone like you would be the apple of his mother's eye,' she said, and Guy lifted an eyebrow.

'Someone like me?'

'I'm sure you're perfectly aware of how good-looking you are,' said Lucy with a touch of spice. 'You can be charming—when you're not being *really* irritating, that is—and you're obviously attentive. I might not appreciate you myself, but I can see that most mothers would adore having a son like you. Some women are grateful if their sons ring them once a month, let alone visit them in the hospital every day.'

Guy had laughed at her comment about him being irritating, but at that he sobered. 'I think my mother is grateful,' he said quietly. 'And she loves me, I know she does. She just can't show it that easily. Remember, she grew up in the outback. It's a tough life out there, and they weren't encouraged to spend a lot of time talking about their emotions, at least not in those days. She's had a hard time, too. When she's brusque, it's just her way of dealing with the fact that she's lost the two people she loved most in the world.'

'Your father…?' Lucy asked, wondering why Guy wasn't the person his mother had always loved most in the world.

'And Michael.' Guy's voice was expressionless. 'My brother. Now, he *was* the apple of my mother's eye. My father's, too. Michael was everything they wanted in a son. He worked hard, he was head boy at school, he was steady and responsible, and never for a moment did he complain about his destiny to take over Dangerfield & Dunn when my father retired. I used to ask him if he didn't want to do something else with his life, to have some fun, but Michael never liked taking risks. He joined the firm as soon as he left university and seemed perfectly happy to go into the office every day. Ironic, really.'

'Why's that?'

'Because it was going in to the office that killed him. It was a hit-and-run accident. He'd been working late—of course—and it was dark, but he was using the zebra crossing, because Michael always did the right thing. It wasn't his fault that joy-riders don't always stop at pedestrian crossings, or that he just happened to be crossing the road as they came round the corner.'

Guy sighed and shook his head. 'He was killed outright.'

'I'm sorry.' Without thinking, Lucy laid her hand over his, where it was resting on his thigh, and Guy turned it so that their palms met and their fingers entwined.

'My parents were never the same again,' he told her. 'My father had a heart attack only months later and left my mother all on her own. They had a very strong marriage, and Ma has been bereft ever since. She retreated into her shell and, whenever she's difficult, I remind myself of what she's still suffering.'

The lazy good humour was so much a part of Guy that it was almost a shock to realise that he had tragedy in his background. She had just assumed that his light-heartedness came from a charmed life, but she had been wrong, Lucy realised with compunction. Guy might be privileged in lots of ways, but there was clearly much more to him than she had thought. He was clearly far from the playboy she had dismissed him as in Australia. It had only taken a day at Dangerfield & Dunn to realise that the staff there held him in respect.

Perhaps she was going to have to change some of her assumptions about him, thought Lucy.

Her fingers tightened around his in unspoken sympathy. 'What about you?' she asked, thinking that he had lost as much as his mother. 'Were you and Michael close?'

Guy shook his head. 'Michael was nearly ten years older than me. I looked up to him, but it was too wide a gap for us ever to be really close. Still, he was my brother.'

He fell silent for a moment and Lucy wondered if he were even aware that they were holding hands.

'Ten years is a big gap,' she commented, not sure what else to say, and Guy glanced at her.

'I think I was a "mistake",' he said, and she was relieved to see the glinting smile reappear. 'Michael was too kind ever to say so, but I worked it out for myself. Even as a small boy I could see that he was all my parents needed. Michael was destined for the family firm, and there was nothing left for me to do but be difficult. It wasn't that I was jealous of him— at least, I don't think I was,' he added with scrupulous honesty. 'I didn't want Michael's life in the bank. I wanted adventure, excitement, something *different*.'

'Hence the rodeo riding?'

He smiled an acknowledgement of her memory. 'Yes, that was an early ambition, but falling off a few horses at Wirrindago soon knocked that one out of me! I conformed enough to go to university, but then I dropped out and bummed around the world for a while, surfing, sailing, skiing, white water rafting…doing anything that took my fancy. I was a free spirit like you once!'

'That can't have gone down very well with your parents,' said Lucy, burningly aware of the warmth and strength of the fingers curled around hers.

'They were appalled at the waste of my expensive education, and I don't blame them,' said Guy. 'They couldn't understand why I wasn't more like Michael, when I'd had all the advantages he had had, but I just wanted to have a good time, and I did. I can't say I regret it at all, although I suspect I did hurt my parents more than I thought. I was pretty selfish.'

'And then Michael died?'

'And then Michael died,' he agreed, his voice carefully expressionless. 'And then my father, and then there was only me to take over.'

Lucy's eyes rested on his profile. 'That must have been hard,' she said quietly.

Guy shrugged off her sympathy. 'I felt sorry enough for myself at the time. The last thing I wanted was to settle down and spend my life being second best, but it would have seemed as if I were letting Pa and Michael down if I didn't, so I hung up my surfboard and came home to knuckle down and do what I could for my mother. And you'll never guess what happened...'

'What?'

'I found I loved it!' The familiar, heart-shaking smile gleamed in the dim light. 'It's not catching a wave but investment banking is all about taking risks, and making money has got an excitement all of its own. The last thing I expected was to enjoy myself, but I must have absorbed more from the old man than I thought I had.

'Not that it's been all that easy,' he went on. 'I've had a struggle with some of the older members of the board, who were used to thinking of me as the young, irresponsible one. It's over four years since I took over, and it's only now that they're starting to accept me. It's the same with Ma in lots of ways,' he said thoughtfully. 'In her mind, I'm still the wild one.'

Lucy nodded. 'Like Meredith is still the sensible one and I'm still the irresponsible one. Do you think we can ever change the way our families think of us?'

'Probably not,' said Guy, 'but we can change the way we think of ourselves.' Looking down, he seemed to realise suddenly that their hands were still linked and he disentangled his fingers from hers with a faint smile. 'We can try, anyway.'

Lucy's hand felt cold and uncomfortable on its own. Not knowing what else to do with it, she set it on her lap like a parcel and stared down at it, half expecting to see it glowing from the way it throbbed and tingled. Afraid that it would start twitching at any minute, she clamped her other hand over it to keep it still as she thought about what Guy had said.

'Is that what my challenge is about?' she asked slowly, and Guy turned his head to look into her face.

'If you want it to be,' he said.

Lucy's first couple of weeks at Dangerfield & Dunn passed so quickly that she was quite surprised to find herself in a packed City bar one Friday night, celebrating the end of a fortnight's employment. Always envious of Lucy's travels, Meg had been very sympathetic about Lucy having to adjust to office life.

'It can't be much fun after working on a cattle station,' she said, raising her voice to be heard as they fought their way to a table. She had the bottle while Lucy held their glasses high to avoid spilling them as they pushed through the crowd. 'Aren't you bored?'

'The funny thing is, I'm not,' said Lucy slowly, setting the glasses on the table.

She had expected to be. Guy's challenge had been to get

the job in the first place, and she herself had vowed that she would make a success of it, but it hadn't occurred to her that she might actually enjoy it. If anything, she had pictured herself pining for the outback, and sticking steadfastly to her vow in spite of it. As things had turned out, she had been too busy to pine.

'I thought being a receptionist would be really dull,' she told Meg. 'I thought it would mean just sitting behind a desk all day, filing my nails, but there's much more to it than that.'

She pushed Meg's glass across to her. 'It's surprising how many different people come through the doors every day and the different things they need to know. Sometimes it's just a question of pointing them in the right direction, but at others they need more practical help. We get a lot of overseas visitors and they often ask for advice about how to get to different parts of London, or how to go about booking something.

'In fact, we seem to be the advice centre for everyone. It's amazing the information Imogen has at her fingertips! How to book theatre tickets, where to get help for everything from a stubbed toe to a divorce, who to talk to about what in the bank, where's the nearest place you can buy mascara—I had that just the other day!—booking taxis…'

She faltered to a halt as she found herself fixed by Meg's accusing stare. 'What?'

'You sound as if you're enjoying it!'

Lucy didn't do nine-to-five and commuting with the rest of them. She was the friend they all relied on to work for wacky organisations, the one who was prepared to pack her bags and move on, who reminded them that it was still possible to chuck it all in if only they dared. For Lucy to take to working in a bank, however temporarily, felt almost like a betrayal to Meg.

'Well…' Lucy was well aware of how uncharacteristically

she was behaving at the moment and she ran her finger round the rim of her glass a little uneasily. 'I suppose I like dealing with people, and there's more scope than I thought to use my initiative. Dangerfield & Dunn is such a friendly place to work, too. It feels as if everyone's got a part to play...even the receptionists!'

'I might try and get a job there myself,' said Meg, impressed in spite of her reservations. 'It sounds as if Guy Dangerfield has a better idea of how to run a company than my bosses! How is the gorgeous Guy, anyway?'

Lucy had told her the bare bones about her return to London with Guy and the night she had spent at his apartment, but Meg knew her very well and was adept at reading between the lines. It hadn't taken her any time to winkle the whole story out of Lucy.

'I've hardly seen him,' Lucy said.

It was true. She had caught occasional glimpses of Guy walking to or from the lifts. He never failed to smile and greet her and Imogen, but he didn't come over and talk to them again, even on the rare occasions when he was on his own.

Lucy didn't *mind*—obviously—but she couldn't help feeling just a little put out. After all, the last time they had spoken, she had held his hand and he had told her about his brother's death. It wasn't the kind of conversation you had with a total stranger, and perhaps he regretted telling her as much as he had, but she hadn't forced him to confide in her, had she?

Meg was watching her as she drank her wine abstractedly. 'Has he kissed you again?'

Lucy flushed. She wished she hadn't told Meg about that. At least she had managed to be fairly casual about it, and Meg had no idea quite how much Guy's kiss had affected her.

'No, as far as he's concerned I'm just the new reception-ist now,' she said as lightly as she could.

'It must be a bit awkward, isn't it?' said Meg. 'Having kissed your boss?'

'He wasn't my boss when I kissed him, and anyway *he* kissed me first. Why should I feel awkward?'

'Maybe Guy does? He might be too embarrassed to talk to you now.'

Lucy gave a short laugh. 'Guy? I can't imagine him being embarrassed about anything!'

'Perhaps he's met someone else?' Meg suggested.

This thought had occurred to Lucy, too, more than once. Imogen, source of all information on Guy, hadn't mentioned anything about a new girlfriend, but presumably she didn't know everything.

'Not as far as I know,' she said. 'Anyway, it doesn't matter to me,' she said with a touch of defiance. 'I'm just there to do my job. Guy can do what he wants.'

Still, it was hard to concentrate on the job when her heart did that ridiculous flip-flop every time she glimpsed Guy striding across the atrium, every time he turned his head and sent them that smile, every time his laugh rang out.

It was strange how one man, dressed exactly like all the others, could change the whole feel of the building. There was no need to hoist a flag to show that Guy Dangerfield was in residence. All were aware of a shift in the air, the sense of an ocean breeze swirling in and blowing away the staleness in the atmosphere, that charge of extra ozone he brought into the room that made everyone sit up straighter.

Lucy felt it too. Try as she might not to notice him, all her senses were on alert the moment he stepped out of the lift. It seemed incredible now that she had once dismissed him as lazy and a lightweight. How could she not have noticed the charisma of the man in Australia? The older members of the board might be resistant to his charms, but to the staff of Dangerfield & Dunn Guy was a hero.

Lucy understood why they admired him, but when she looked at him now, she didn't just see the successful banker with an inclusive approach and a thoughtful word for the least significant of his staff. She saw the lonely child with the elder brother who seemed to give his parents everything they needed. She saw the boy dreaming of being a rodeo rider, the young man kicking against convention, the surfer on the crest of a wave, the wind in his hair and the sun in his eyes. The man who had given up his freedom because he didn't want to let his father down.

The man who walked past her now as if she had never kissed him on the quayside, had never held his hand in the dark.

'I'll probably never hear from him again,' she told Meg. 'Anyway, it's Friday. Why don't I get another bottle?'

CHAPTER SIX

GUY rang the next day. 'Have I got you at a bad time?' he said.

'Er...no...I'm just buying some shoes.' Lucy had answered the phone without thinking, assuming that it would be Meg arranging where to meet for lunch, and the sound of his voice set her heart thumping wildly against her ribs. Her knees felt suddenly, ridiculously, weak too, and she sat down abruptly on the nearest stool, oblivious to the shoppers around her.

'Not glass slippers, by any chance?'

'No.' Lucy looked down at the shoes on her feet. They were a practical black, the heel sturdier and not as high as Meg's turquoise shoes, but they had an elegant shape and Lucy loved the floppy bow they boasted. 'Some sensible shoes to wear to work.'

'Sensible? That doesn't sound like you, Cinders,' said Guy, the old laugh back in his voice, and she could picture him with alarming clarity, holding the phone to his ear, the blue eyes dancing, his cheek creasing with his smile.

'You challenged me to change,' she pointed out. 'Maybe I have changed enough to invest in comfortable shoes.'

'I'll know when I see them,' he said.

Lucy took a breath and made herself sound brisk. 'What can I do for you?'

'My mother is at home and in urgent need of distraction,' he said, getting down to business. 'You did say once that you'd be prepared to talk to her about Wirrindago one day.'

'I remember.' It wasn't too much to spend a couple of hours distracting an elderly lady from her pain, Lucy thought. 'Did you want to arrange a time for me to go round?'

'I don't suppose you could make tomorrow afternoon?' said Guy hopefully.

'I said I would go and see Richard in the evening, but around teatime would be fine.'

Meg was delighted to hear that Guy had insisted on coming to pick Lucy up. 'I can't wait to meet him,' she said excitedly. 'What are you going to wear?'

'It's not a date, Meg. I'm just going to have tea with his mother.'

'Yes, and how many guys—if you'll excuse the pun—introduce you to their mothers unless they're really interested?' retorted Meg. 'You could wear your new shoes.'

But Lucy was determined not to make an effort. That would suggest that she was excited at the thought of seeing Guy again and treating it like a date, when she was just a cook from Wirrindago going to have tea with his mother. So she put on her old jeans and a T-shirt, and if the pale blue cardigan she threw over the top happened to be her softest and most flattering one, that was just because it was the first one to hand and certainly not because she had chosen it specially.

Guy was driving himself this time and turned up in—what else?—a Porsche that made Meg's eyes pop as she peered through the front window. Annoyingly, he had managed to park right outside the house. 'Ooh, he must be seriously rich to have one of those.' Meg whistled, impressed. 'If you don't want him, Lucy, can I have him?' She hurried to the door. 'I'll go and let him in.'

Lucy was left, desperately trying to get her breathing under control. In the hallway she could hear Guy charming Meg, and the sound of his voice sent the butterflies in her stomach into a frenzy. Anyone would think that she was nervous, she chastised herself as she got to her feet, appalled to find that her legs were doing a passable imitation of jelly. It was only Guy, she reminded herself sternly. There had been a time when she couldn't have cared less if Meg was flirting with him.

Then Guy appeared in the doorway and instantly every particle of oxygen was sucked from the air, and it seemed to Lucy that her heart actually stopped for a moment. His presence in the tiny room was overwhelming and his smile was like a jolt of adrenalin, setting every cell in her body on high alert.

Desperately, Lucy forced her lungs back into working mode. *Breathe in, breathe out. Remember?*

'Hi,' she said.

Fortunately Guy didn't seem to notice that her voice was all over the place. It was amazing how much wavering up and down the register you could fit into such a short word. Thank goodness she hadn't tried anything longer, like good afternoon.

'Show me your new shoes,' he said. 'I want to see how much you've changed.'

He studied them with interest when Lucy reappeared in the shoes. 'What do you think?' she asked, pointing her toes.

'Very nice.' Guy glanced up at her and smiled, and Lucy's heart duly performed a breathless somersault. Pathetic.

'I've been borrowing Meg's shoes, but they've all got such high heels that I could barely walk by the end of the week,' she told him, horribly afraid that she was babbling but unable to stop it. 'I thought I should buy some of my own, so I took your advice and asked for a small advance on my salary.'

For some reason it seemed important to let him know that she wasn't relying on her friend more than she had to. She hadn't forgotten his comment about the way she let everyone else look after her. 'That way I don't have to keep borrowing off Meg.'

She had put some money aside already to pay Meg rent for her room too, although she knew that her friend would insist that it wasn't necessary. What with buying shoes and taking control of finances, really, she was turning into Susan Sensible.

'I could only afford one pair, so I had to get shoes that went with everything.' Lucy regarded them dubiously. 'Black isn't as much fun as other colours, but it's more practical, I suppose.'

Guy's eyes gleamed as he inspected them. 'You've done well, Cinders. You've managed to buy sensible shoes that are sexy at the same time. I like the bows too. They show a sense of fun.' He looked back up at Lucy. 'I'd say these shoes still have a lot of you in them, though. That sensible side is new, but the rest of it is still definitely you. You've changed, but not too much. That's good.'

A blush crept up Lucy's cheeks and she sat down abruptly, bending her head to hide her face as she made a big deal of pulling off the shoes and shoving her feet into her faithful trainers instead. Hoping her normal colour would have returned by then, she stood up. 'We'd better go,' she said.

'So, how is your challenge going?' asked Guy as he manoeuvred the car out of the tight parking space. 'I hear reception is a very different place since you've been working there.'

Was that good or bad? Lucy wondered. 'I like my job,' she admitted cautiously. 'More than I thought I would. And everyone is very friendly.'

He glanced at her as he waited to turn into the main road. 'That's what they say about you, too.'

'Me?' she said blankly.

'I understand you've set up a counselling service in reception?'

Lucy flushed slightly. 'Oh, that was just someone who seemed very upset when she arrived. Her boyfriend had dumped her without warning, and she was obviously in a state. We rang up to her department to say that she'd been a bit delayed and I made her a coffee and let her talk for a bit until she calmed down—but it was only for a few minutes,' she told Guy in case he thought she had been wasting company time. 'And Imogen was on the desk all the time.'

'I'm not angry with you—far from it,' he said. 'She wouldn't have been able to concentrate if she'd spent the day bottling up her feelings and, as it was, she managed a meeting with me and the head of her department. She told me afterwards that you'd really helped her.'

'I didn't do anything,' said Lucy uncomfortably. 'I just listened.'

'Sometimes that's all the help you need,' said Guy. 'Sometimes all you want is a friendly smile when you come in the door, or someone who can see what needs to be done and gets on with it without waiting to be told.' He smiled at her as they drew up to some traffic lights and he put the car into neutral gear. 'You're doing a good job.'

Lucy actually blushed. 'I didn't think you really noticed us on reception.'

'I always notice you,' said Guy.

Bridget Dangerfield lived in an enormous house in Belgravia with a white stucco front. 'It's much too big for her,' said Guy as he locked the car. 'I've been trying to persuade her to move but she won't hear of it.'

He let himself in the imposing front door, calling a 'hallo' to announce their arrival, and led Lucy up the stairs to the first floor. Bridget was waiting at the top, leaning on two sticks. She was a handsome woman, tall and shrewd-eyed, and her big hands were adorned with some spectacular diamond rings.

'You shouldn't have got up, Ma,' said Guy, kissing her on the cheek.

'Of course I need to get up,' she snapped at him. 'I've never welcomed a guest sitting down and I'm not going to start now. Besides, I'm supposed to be practising getting in and out of my chair.'

She turned her attention to Lucy, eyeing her appraisingly as Guy made the introductions. 'So you're Lucy?' she said. 'Hmm. Guy was right. You're very pretty.'

'Sorry, did I hear that right?' Guy grinned at his mother, pretending astonishment. *'Guy was right.* I've never heard you say that before! Are you feeling quite well, Ma?'

'I don't have much cause to say it often,' she retorted, but Lucy thought there was a hint of a smile in her face.

'You'd better come in.' Moving slowly and carefully on her sticks, Bridget led the way into a beautifully furnished draw-ing room that spanned the entire width of the house. 'Would you like some tea?' she asked Lucy.

'That would be lovely,' said Lucy. 'Can I help?'

'Why don't I get the tea?' Guy began, but Bridget rounded on him.

'I'm not gaga!' she said irritably. 'It's my hips that have been replaced, not my brain or my hands! I'm perfectly capa-ble of boiling a kettle. Lucy can come with me and carry the tray. She'll probably want to stretch her legs if she's been trapped in that ridiculous car of yours. It's—'

'Far too small and far too fast, I know, Ma.' Guy grinned affectionately at his mother. It was obviously an old argument.

'You go and make the tea, then, but no telling Lucy any embarrassing stories about my potty training days, OK?'

He settled himself comfortably on a sofa as Bridget snorted and shook her head.

'He will *fuss*,' she told Lucy as they made their painstaking way to the kitchen. 'And he's always interfering. He's been turning everything upside down while I was in hospital! New chair, new bed, new railings everywhere,' she grumbled. 'And then he went and employed a nurse! I soon got rid of *her*.'

Harrumphing, she indicated that Lucy should fill up the kettle. 'Anyone would think I was sick!' she said in outraged tones that held only the faintest hint of her Australian background after so many years in England.

'I'm sure Guy just wants you to be comfortable,' said Lucy, who was beginning to think that he had much greater reserves of patience than she had guessed. In spite of her insistence to the contrary, it was clear that his mother couldn't make the tea and hold on to her sticks without a great deal of difficulty, and in the end it was Lucy who set out the cups and saucers, found the milk and the biscuits and warmed the pot, all under Bridget's eagle-eyed direction.

'I suppose he told you this place is too big for me, too,' said Bridget with a grouchy look.

'I can see why he might think that you'd be better off somewhere a little more...practical,' Lucy said cautiously, thinking of all the stairs.

'I've lived here all my married life. I'm not moving. I let Guy put this kitchen in here so I didn't have to go up and down stairs all the time, but that's enough and so you can tell Guy.'

Lucy looked up from the teapot, suddenly afraid that she might have got hold of quite the wrong end of the stick. 'You know that Guy and I aren't...' she began awkwardly.

'Yes, yes, he told me.' Bridget waved her stick in vague

acknowledgement. 'He said you were practically engaged to a stockman at Wirrindago. He sounds *most* unsuitable,' she went on with a stringent look. 'It's a hard life as a stockman's wife, Lucy. You'd be much better off with Guy.'

'Oh, I don't…there's really no question…' stammered Lucy, horrified in case she had somehow given the wrong impression.

'You could do worse,' said Bridget, ignoring her completely. 'I'm not saying he can't be a bit silly at times, but no more than any other man. He didn't have an easy time as a child,' she said with a quick sidelong glance at Lucy. 'Guy was one of those boys who always seem to be fine and happy, but you never really know what's going on in their heads. You think they're all right, but they'll tell a joke rather than show their feelings.

'There are some biscuits in the tin up there,' she interrupted herself. 'No, the blue one… Still, Guy's a good man, and he'd be a good father,' she told Lucy, who didn't know what on earth to say. 'He needs someone to take him seriously, and then maybe he would take himself more seriously, and who knows what he could achieve then?'

'He's achieved a lot already,' Lucy found herself saying as she opened the tin. 'The staff at Dangerfield & Dunn think he's wonderful.'

Bridget looked at her with an odd little smile. 'And you?'

Lucy set out the biscuits on the plate, unable to meet the older woman's eyes for some reason. 'I'm just temporary,' she said.

In the end, the tea was much more relaxed than Lucy had feared. They talked mostly about Wirrindago, a place they all loved. Guy and Lucy might have been there most recently, but it was Bridget who knew the outback best, and Lucy enjoyed listening to her stories, although all the while she was conscious of Guy lounging nearby, of his lazy smile and the glinting humour in his eyes.

Quite unfazed by his mother's abruptness, he teased her affectionately and made her snort with laughter occasionally. Watching carefully, Lucy noticed that Bridget's eyes softened when they rested on Guy when she thought that no one was looking. Bridget, she suspected, hid her real feelings behind brusqueness just as her son did behind humour.

'So, there's no sign of Hal getting married yet?' she demanded, shaking her head. 'He's as bad as you, Guy. What is he now, thirty-four? Thirty-five? It's high time he found himself a wife.'

'Wives aren't that easy to come by in the outback, Ma.'

'That's not an excuse *you* have,' Bridget countered. 'There are plenty of girls in London!'

'True, but it's hard to find the right one,' said Guy.

'There must be lots of nice girls out there. Look at Lucy here!'

'Sadly, Lucy is spoken for,' he said easily. He grinned at Lucy. 'Don't tell me she's been matchmaking again!'

'I just want you to be happy,' said Bridget grouchily.

'I know you do, Ma.' Guy's voice was very gentle. 'But I want what you and Dad had. You wouldn't really want me to settle for less than that, would you?'

Lucy's heart twisted as she saw Bridget's eyes fill with tears. 'No,' she muttered, and the hand that lifted her cup shook a little as she tried furiously to blink away the signs of her weakness.

There was a tiny pause. 'I should go,' said Lucy tactfully and put down her own cup and saucer. 'Thank you so much for tea. I've really enjoyed it.'

'It's been lovely to have you.' Bridget insisted on struggling out of her chair and on to her sticks to see them to the top of the stairs. 'Thank you for coming, Lucy. I hope Guy will bring you again—or come on your own!'

'I'd like that,' said Lucy sincerely, and on an impulse kissed Bridget on the cheek.

'Thank you so much, Lucy,' said Guy as he closed the front door behind them with a heartfelt sigh. 'You were wonderful. Ma really liked you, I could tell.'

'I liked her too. She's quite a character, isn't she?'

'And I'm sorry about all the matchmaking,' he said, although the blue eyes were dancing. 'She doesn't usually try and marry guests off to me on their first visit!'

Take it lightly, Lucy told herself. 'I should be honoured then.'

'You should indeed.' He grinned at her as he unlocked the car. 'I'm afraid you've definitely moved to the top of her list! Get in,' he added. 'I'll drive you to the hospital.'

'I can easily get a bus,' Lucy began, but it was a pretty feeble effort and she found herself climbing meekly back into the car.

'It's the least I can do after today,' said Guy. 'I'm not brave enough to tell my mother I let you go off in the bus, and besides, my only alternative is to stay and be lectured about how I should be persuading you to marry me straight away.' He shook his head as the engine purred into life. 'I love my mother dearly but sometimes…well, let's just say she can be a bit trying!'

Lucy pulled her phone out of her bag and made a pretence of checking it for messages while she tried not to think about Guy persuading her to marry him. It was nonsense of course, but…what *would* it be like?

'I'm sure she can be difficult,' she said, wondering if she could tell Guy that she thought his mother knew him much better than he imagined, and that she loved him much more than she showed, but it seemed presumptuous under the circumstances. If she really were going to marry Guy, it would be different, of course. She could say it if she were his fiancée.

Which she wasn't.

'You're lucky to have her,' she said instead, dropping the mobile back into the bag at her feet. 'I wish I had a mother, even a difficult one!'

'I'm sorry,' said Guy. 'When did she die?'

'I was only three,' Lucy told him. 'I don't really remember her at all, but I wish I'd known her. In the photos we've got, she always looks like fun.'

'You lost your mother when you were three?' Guy was horrified. 'You poor little kid. What about your father?'

'He remarried a couple of years later. Our stepmother is perfectly nice, but it's Meredith who brought me up really, even though she's only a couple of years older. She was the one constant presence in my life. Dad was posted overseas when I was only seven and we had to go to boarding school but Meredith was always there if I needed her.'

Guy glanced at her. 'And Meredith is the reason you're still visiting Richard so faithfully. You're doing it for her.'

'Yes.' Lucy nodded even though it wasn't a question. 'He's getting better, thank goodness, so at least I've had some good news to email her. He can't talk for long, but he's definitely on the mend.

'The thing is,' she went on slowly, 'I think Meredith is wrong. Richard always seems happy to see me, but if he did love me before the accident, I think he's forgotten about it now. I mean, you *know* when someone loves you, don't you?'

'Do you?' Guy's voice was very level. 'You usually know when they *don't,* certainly.'

'Well, I don't think Richard does,' said Lucy. 'It's a bit of a relief, to be honest. I don't think he's going to be hurt when he finds out I'm leaving again.' She sighed. 'I just wish he'd get well enough to tell his parents that. They've been making a few comments recently about how elusive my boyfriend is, and I suspect they're hoping the relationship has fallen through, which will leave me free to make Richard happy.'

'You'll have to tell them you and Guy are still madly in love,' said Guy, pulling up right outside the hospital entrance.

'I've tried, believe me.' Lucy unclipped her seat belt and turned to him. 'Thanks for the lift,' she said with a smile, desperate not to let him guess how much all this talk of love unsettled her. 'I'll tell them Guy dropped me off tonight. Maybe that will seem more convincing.'

'You know what would be much more convincing, don't you, Lucy?'

And then she made a big mistake. She looked directly at Guy. Now her eyes were all tangled up with his, and her heart had braked until it was no more than a sluggish beat, each stroke a slow, painful slam in her chest.

Lucy struggled to stay calm, but it was hard when her body only seemed to be able to manage one function at a time. If she jerked her eyes away, her heart stopped. If she concentrated on keeping her heart beating, her lungs forgot how to work and she found herself struggling for breath. It was hopeless.

'What?' she asked, but it came out as a whisper.

'I think it would be much more convincing if you went in looking as if you had been thoroughly kissed by your lover,' said Guy, his voice reverberating deep and quiet, and he reached out and traced the outline of her mouth with his thumb, a touch so tantalising that Lucy closed her eyes instinctively against the sharp twist of response inside her. 'What do you think?' His voice dropped even further.

'I...I'm not...' How was she expected to *think* when his other hand was sliding beneath her hair, tugging gently at the back of her neck to bring her towards him? When every nerve in her body was sighing, *Yes, say yes! Say you think it's the best idea you've ever heard*. When her blood was singing and her lips were tingling with anticipation and she wanted, more than anything, to close the gap between them and kiss him again.

And then the gap was closed anyway, and his mouth was on hers and hers was on his and the sensations exploded inside her, shattering the last feeble attempt to be sensible and releasing deep-honeyed delight that made her murmur with pleasure and curl her palm around his jaw. She could feel the faint prickle of golden stubble beneath her fingers and his smile curving against her lips and, deep down, the simmer of a lurking excitement that would erupt if they weren't careful.

Perhaps Guy felt it, too. Reluctantly, he lifted his head and smiled down into Lucy's face. Her cheeks were flushed, her blue eyes dazed and dreamy, her lips curved voluptuously, and he risked one more kiss as he smoothed some golden strands of hair behind her ears.

'That's better,' he said. 'You look like a girl in love now.'

This was just a game to Guy. The truth struck Lucy like a blow and she jerked back. That lovely kiss, the warmth and the sweetness, meant nothing to him. He had just been teasing her, playing with her. Look at his eyes, dancing with laughter. He thought it was *funny*.

'Let's hope it does the trick, then,' she said. She longed to sound cool, but her voice wasn't that steady. She fumbled for the door handle. 'It would be a shame if all that was for nothing, wouldn't it?'

'Lucy—' Guy began, but she was already grabbing her bag and clambering out of the car, slamming the door shut behind her when she finally managed to disentangle herself. Bridget was right. It *was* a stupid design.

And then Lucy was stalking away towards the hospital entrance, so blind with a mixture of fury and disappointment and frustration that she didn't notice the man tucking a mobile phone into his jacket pocket until she had walked right into him.

'I am *so* sorry…' she apologised breathlessly, and then broke off. 'Frank?'

'Lucy!' said Richard's father, sounding equally surprised. 'What are you doing out here? Is everything OK?'

'Yes, I just came out to make a couple of calls. You know they won't let us use mobiles in the hospital.' He looked more closely at her flushed face and stormy eyes. 'Are you all right, Lucy?'

Lucy opened her mouth to tell him that no, she was *not* all right. She had just been kissed by someone so insufferably smug, conceited, patronising and *infuriating* that he actually thought it was funny to turn her inside out and upside down and then laugh at her.

But they were interrupted before she could get started. 'Lucy! You forgot your—' Guy was getting out of the car with her mobile in his hand, calling to catch her attention before he registered that she was talking to someone she knew '—phone,' he finished. 'It must have fallen out of your bag.'

'Oh.' It would have been nice to have been able to tell him exactly where he could stuff the phone but, unfortunately, she needed it. 'Thank you,' she said stiffly, holding out her hand for it as Guy came up.

To her surprise, she saw Frank looking from Guy to her and then back again with a very odd expression on his face. There didn't seem much choice but to introduce the two men and, since Guy was here, he might as well make himself useful. Surely meeting him in the flesh would convince Frank and Ellen that he was real at last—and a lot more effectively than a kiss!

'Frank, this is Guy Dangerfield,' she said, a little puzzled by the astonishment in Frank's face.

'Guy?' he echoed. '*Your* Guy?'

'Er…yes,' said Lucy with a glance at Guy, whose face was carefully expressionless. What was going on? 'Guy, as you've probably gathered, this is Richard's father, Frank Pollard.'

Guy offered Frank his hand. 'I was very sorry to hear about your son's accident,' he said, 'but I gather that he's on the road to recovery now.'

'He is, thank you…yes…' Frank stammered. 'My goodness,' he said, positively overwhelmed. 'What a pleasure to meet you! This is a bit of a surprise, I must say. No wonder Lucy has been so secretive about you.'

Frank turned to Lucy and wagged a jovial finger at her. 'You never told us you were involved with Guy Dangerfield!'

'I did!' Lucy was completely mystified by his reaction. 'I was always talking about him!'

'You just said Guy. We didn't realise you meant Guy *Dangerfield.*'

Guy's slightly wooden expression relaxed as he watched Lucy, who clearly didn't have a clue what Frank was talking about. 'You're not ashamed of me, are you, darling?' he said, and she glared at him, not trusting him an inch when he had that glint in his eye.

'Of course not, *darling,*' she replied, baring her teeth at him. 'How could I possibly be ashamed of *you?*' She turned back to Frank. 'Have you met before?'

'Me? No! I've just read about Guy here,' said Frank hastily. 'He's a very well-respected figure in the business community—famous, in fact. But you must know that, Lucy.'

Guy put an arm around Lucy. 'Lucy isn't interested in the business pages, are you, sweetheart?'

'Still, you must have realised that we'd have heard about Guy,' said Frank, fortunately not noticing that Lucy was looking daggers at Guy at the time. 'Well, well, well! And all the time you were here, you were going home to Guy Dangerfield and you never said a thing!'

'That's because he's just Guy to me.' Lucy even managed a simper as she snuggled into Guy and fluttered her lashes up at him, but only Guy could see that behind the sweet pose her blue eyes were bright with challenge.

Obviously he was a lot more famous than she had realised. Lucy was not, in fact, a great reader of the papers, but she didn't need Guy pointing that out. She had recognised the respect in which he was held at Dangerfield & Dunn, but she hadn't understood that he had a wider influence. Frank was carrying on as if he were Bill Gates! Meg hadn't recognised him, but then Meg's knowledge of the business world wasn't much greater than her own. She would know if a chain of shoe shops had been the subject of a hostile takeover, perhaps, but that would be it.

'It didn't seem right to talk about how happy we were when Richard was so ill,' she went on, feeling that she had a score to settle with Guy. He had claimed that kiss had been all about convincing Frank and Ellen that she really did have a lover. Well, she would make things even more convincing, and see how he liked that! 'But of course, now he's getting better, we don't need to keep it secret any longer.'

Guy's arm was like iron around her and she felt it stiffen, as if he could sense where she was leading. Lucy smiled adoringly up at him, rather enjoying herself now. 'I can tell Frank, can't I, darling? We've just come from Guy's mother,' she went on without waiting for his reply. 'We wanted her to be the first to know.'

'You mean…?' Frank looked from one to the other, his evident incredulity scarcely flattering, she couldn't help thinking crossly. What did he think—that she wasn't good enough for the great Guy Dangerfield?

'Yes.' Her downcast lashes and demure smile were perfect. 'We're going to get married!'

CHAPTER SEVEN

LUCY HEARD GUY suck in his breath, but she deliberately ignored him. 'We were going to keep it within the family for now,' she told Frank, 'but since it's you... You don't mind if the Pollards know, do you, Guy?'

'Of course not,' said Guy after the tiniest of pauses. 'But, as Lucy says, we don't want to make this public yet. I'm sure you understand,' he added smoothly.

'Oh, yes, yes, of *course*. Mum's the word.' Frank was clearly unsure how to take this unexpected development. Flabbergasted wouldn't be too strong a word to describe his demeanour. 'This is all a bit of a surprise.'

'Isn't it?' agreed Guy, a certain rigidity in his smile as Lucy snuggled closer, pleased with his reaction. Let him be on the receiving end of a joke for once!

'I can't say we hadn't hoped that Lucy and Richard would...but of course we're happy for you, Lucy,' said Frank, kissing her gallantly on the cheek. 'I know Ellen will be too. Richard may be a bit more disappointed but...well...as long as you're happy.'

Privately, Lucy was convinced that Richard wouldn't care nearly as much as his parents seemed to think, but there was no point in saying that to Frank.

'Thank you, Frank. That's sweet of you,' she said, kissing him back.

Frank turned to Guy and wrung his hand. 'Congratulations! You're a lucky man!'

'I know. I can hardly believe it myself,' said Guy, his voice laden with irony that only Lucy seemed able to hear. 'It hardly seems real yet!'

'Come up and meet Richard and Ellen,' Frank was urging, but fortunately Guy managed a graceful refusal. 'I can't leave the car where it is. I'm liable to get towed away as it is, I'm afraid,' he said. 'I really just came to drop Lucy off.'

'Oh, that's a shame. Another time, maybe. You're coming in, though, Lucy?'

'Of course.' Deciding that she had probably pushed Guy far enough, Lucy opted for a tactical retreat. 'I'll come with you.' She kissed the corner of Guy's mouth. 'Bye, darling!' she said gaily and waggled her fingers at him in farewell. 'See you tomorrow!'

And tucking her hand into Frank's arm, she sashayed off with him, leaving Guy looking after her with a twisted smile on his face.

'I can't believe it!' cried Richard's mother when Frank broke the news. 'You and *Guy Dangerfield?*'

Lucy accepted Ellen's hug, uneasily aware of the petite blonde nurse called Mairi who was at Richard's bedside, taking his pulse. Mairi seemed to take her pulse-taking duties very seriously. She was always there, holding his wrist and pursing her lips as she checked the watch pinned to her uniform. Lucy felt frivolous next to her, and she could never shake the feeling that Mairi disapproved of her, but she couldn't see why the nurse should be interested in her supposed engagement.

'Yes, it's true, but we want to keep it a secret for now,' she said firmly. It occurred to her that they might want some reason why she and Guy weren't shouting their love from their rooftops. 'We're waiting until Meredith comes back from Australia.'

'Let's hope that's soon,' said Richard as Mairi gave him back his arm. 'I miss her, and you'll want to get married as soon as you can, I expect.' He smiled weakly up at Lucy. 'I'm really happy for you, Lucy.'

In spite of their evident disappointment that she and Richard weren't going to get back together, Ellen and Frank insisted on celebrating her supposed engagement, and took her out for a meal after they had said goodnight to Richard. Their kindness made Lucy feel awful. She shouldn't be lying to them.

It was all Guy's fault, she thought darkly. If he hadn't kissed her, she wouldn't have been provoked into telling Frank that they were engaged. Now she had the sinking feeling that things were getting out of control. The Pollards were alarmingly impressed by the idea of her knowing Guy Dangerfield, let alone marrying him, and the more they talked excitedly about his business reputation, his celebrity status and his fortune, the more Lucy's heart sank. Why had no one told her how famous Guy was?

Why hadn't she listened more closely to Imogen? Or bothered to read a newspaper?

Because you always rely on someone else to sort things out for you.

It wasn't a comfortable thought. Lucy lay awake that night and thought about the times she had blundered into situations without really thinking them through and, although she had never consciously relied on someone else to clear up the mess, maybe that was what had happened. The jobs she had drifted in and out of…had she ever given a thought to the way someone else had to take over from her? She had wild enthusiasms that didn't last. How often did she finish anything she had started, in fact? Lucy wriggled uneasily beneath the duvet.

And what about relationships? Since she was squirming under the lash of self-awareness, she might as well face up to the fact that she had a pattern there, too. Time and again, she had fallen madly in love, only to find that the relationship turned out to be a lot less romantic than she had hoped. It was always fine at first, but when Lucy looked back she realised that she had always been the one to make all the running. She was full of dreams and romance, and the men in question weren't going to turn down a girl with her looks, but how many of them had loved her for herself? she wondered now.

And how much, really, had *she* loved them? Lucy asked herself with sudden insight. Hadn't she just fallen for an image as much as they had done? Look at Kevin. She had been so taken up with the romance of the outback and falling for a man who fitted the part so perfectly that she hadn't paid much attention to what he was really like. No wonder Kevin hadn't seemed bothered when she had had to leave so suddenly. He had understood, better than she had done, that what they had was no more than the romance of a moment.

And now Meredith was stuck in the outback because she, Lucy, had insisted that romance was real. Meredith would be hating every moment, but she had stayed for her sister. Lucy bit her lip at her own selfishness. She would have to go back as soon as she could and rescue Meredith for once.

But first she would have to sort out this latest mess she had got herself into. Lucy wasn't quite sure how to do that, other than by apologising to Guy, and once she had decided on that she managed to convince herself that the situation wasn't that bad. Yes, it had been a stupid thing to say that they were engaged, but there was no reason to believe that it would go any further. Only the Pollards knew about their supposed engagement, and she hoped that she had impressed on them the need for secrecy.

Still, the thought of facing Guy the next day made her feel more than a little nervous and she made a point of getting in to work early. Guy, though, was in even earlier. Lucy had only just hung up her coat and settled down behind the desk when the phone rang.

It was Guy's PA, Sheila, who said that Guy would like to see Lucy at her earliest convenience. Would she come up to his office?

Feeling as if she had been summoned to the headmaster's office, Lucy took one of the spectacular glass lifts up to the penthouse floor. She had never been there before, and would normally have been interested to see what it was like, but now she was too nervous to notice much as she stepped out of the lift.

She wondered what Guy had told Sheila, but it was obviously not the truth, judging by the smile Sheila gave her when she arrived. Grey-haired and very elegant, Sheila adored Guy and was fiercely protective of him. Lucy had helped her out on a couple of occasions, but she knew that wouldn't count for much if Sheila found out that she had been doing anything to prejudice Guy's reputation.

Like pretending to be engaged to him.

'Go right in.' Sheila smiled. 'He's expecting you.'

Taking a deep breath, Lucy pushed open the door of Guy's office, only to stop dead as she stepped inside. It was a huge room with a carpet so deep and soft you could lose yourself in it, a vast desk and some plush sofas where no doubt millions of dollars changed hands regularly in the course of a conversation. One entire wall was made of glass and offered such a spectacular view of St Paul's Cathedral that Lucy actually gasped. 'Oh,' she said, nerves and guilt and embarrassment momentarily forgotten as she stared.

'Quite a view, isn't it?' Guy got up from behind the desk and came towards her and a strange thing happened. The amazing cityscape behind him blurred and he snapped into focus. Everything about him was suddenly sharply defined—the dark blond hair, the planes of his face, the angle of his jaw, those blue, blue eyes with their fan of laughter lines, and Lucy's breath snarled in her throat.

'You sent for me?' It came out more aggressively than she had intended and he raised an eyebrow, gesturing her to one of the sofas.

'I *asked* if you would come and see me,' he corrected her. Hitching up immaculate trousers, he sat down opposite her. 'I could have come to you, I know, but I didn't think you would want to discuss our supposed engagement in the middle of reception. And I think we *do* need to discuss it, don't you?'

'Look, I'm sorry, OK?' said Lucy, guilt making her belligerent. 'I shouldn't have said that to Frank.'

'I seem to remember you promising to think before you opened your mouth,' said Guy mildly enough, but there was something daunting about the set of his mouth, and Lucy could feel dull colour creeping up her throat.

'I might have remembered if I hadn't been provoked!' she retorted.

'Provoked?'

'You know what I mean,' she said sullenly. 'You kissed me.'

The thought of that kiss thickened Lucy's throat and throbbed deep inside her, tingling over her skin and tightening the base of her spine. She was sitting there, not even touching him, and it was as if she could still feel his lips, so warm, so sure, still taste his mouth, still shiver with the pleasure of pressing into his hard, solid body.

'You're right,' said Guy after a moment. 'I shouldn't have done that. I think we both behaved rather badly yesterday. The question is, what do we do about it now?'

'Do we need to do anything? It was a stupid thing for me to say, but nobody knows about it except the Pollards.' Lucy wondered briefly if she should mention Richard's nurse. But why on earth would Mairi be interested in her supposed engagement, let alone go running off to the papers with the news? 'They're not the type to tattle to tabloids, if that's what you're worried about.'

'It had crossed my mind that it would be awkward if the news got out.'

'Why should it, and anyway, why would they be interested in you?' said Lucy. 'I realise that Frank thinks you're some kind of superstar but, to be honest, I'd never heard of you, and I can't see the rest of the world being that bothered either. Who cares if you're getting married or not?'

'My mother?' suggested Guy. 'My friends, my board…and that's just for starters.'

'I can understand your mother wanting to know, but why should your board care?'

Guy got restlessly to his feet and paced behind the sofa. 'It just happens that we're at a delicate stage of negotiation with another bank, with a view to a possible merger,' he explained, choosing his words carefully. 'It's a deal that could transform the way we do business, but it hangs on the decision of their chairman, Bill Sheldon. Personality and trust play a huge part in these kinds of negotiations and, however much he thinks he's making a business decision, he's still going to be influenced by what he thinks of me. I'd rather he didn't associate me with irresponsibility or unpredictability in any way.'

'Oh, pooh, why shouldn't you get engaged if you want to?'

He sighed. 'The point is that I *don't* want to.'

'This Bill doesn't know that, though, does he? You could be an incredibly romantic type who's fallen madly in love with me at first sight and swept me off my feet.'

'That's precisely the impression I don't want to give,' said Guy dryly. 'I want Bill to think of me as steady and responsible, not an impulsive romantic.'

'He's not going to know anything about our engagement,' said Lucy, getting up from the sofa, too. 'The Pollards won't tell anyone, you won't tell anyone, and I won't tell anyone. It's not going to be a problem.'

Guy looked at her, amusement warring with exasperation in his blue eyes. 'I hope you're right.'

Lucy wasn't quite as confident as she sounded, but when two days had passed without any hint of a rumour, she began to relax and believe that no more would be heard of it. She would leave it a week or so and then tell the Pollards that her engagement to Guy was off, she decided as she swiped her card at the ticket gate and joined the press of people heading down the escalator for the Central Line the next morning. They probably wouldn't even be surprised, given that they clearly believed him to be well out of her league.

That was one problem sorted, anyway, she thought with relief. Now she just had to prove to Guy that she was capable of being responsible, and get Meredith back from Wirrindago. Lucy had admitted to herself that she wasn't that desperate to go back to the outback yet. She was embarrassed whenever she thought about how obvious she had made her crush on Kevin, who was little more than a vague romantic memory now, and she was enjoying being in London in a way that she never had before.

Previously she had always been looking for reasons to leave, but it felt different this time. She liked being one of the crowd going in to work. She liked the way the commuters surged in and out of the city like a tide. She liked going out for a sandwich at lunchtime and reading the free newspaper on the tube. She liked meeting friends for a drink in busy bars and pressing her nose up against the windows of all the famous shops where she would never dare walk in, let alone be able to afford to buy anything.

She was even liking work. Reception work wasn't brain surgery, it was true, but she was learning that there was satisfaction in doing a job well, however unimportant it might seem.

The only thing that she didn't like was the way Guy seemed to be ignoring her again. She had barely seen him over the past two days and she wondered if he were crosser with her about their supposed engagement than he had let on. She missed the glint in his blue eyes and the laughter in his voice and the way everything seemed sharper and clearer when he was around. She even missed the annoying way he called her Cinders.

The phone was ringing as Lucy arrived at Dangerfield & Dunn and she picked it up from the other side of the reception desk before she had even taken off her coat.

It was Sheila, Guy's PA, calling from Wales. Her elderly father had fallen the previous evening, she told Lucy, and she was on her way to see him in hospital. She hadn't been able to reach Guy yet, she said.

'The thing is, he's got a series of really important meetings today and he'll need some information that's still on my computer. And there's a reception tonight…someone needs to contact the caterers…'

Lucy shrugged off her coat and reached for a pen. 'Tell me what needs to be done, Sheila, and I'll sort it out.'

There was no one else around as Lucy made her way to Sheila's office, and she allowed herself a spin on the desk chair. It was very quiet up here. What would it be like to have an office to oneself? she wondered. To have a job that you could do well, and to really understand how everything in the organisation worked, as opposed to getting by on charm and hoping for the best?

Not that she was ever likely to know. She couldn't see herself ever having a proper job. With a little sigh, Lucy switched on the computer and typed in the password Sheila had given her.

There was still no sign of Guy by the time she had worked her way through Sheila's list of instructions and printed everything out, so she rummaged through some drawers until she found a file and went to leave the information on his desk.

The huge office felt empty without him. Drawn by the spectacular view of the cathedral, Lucy went over to the glass wall and stood looking down at the city, the file clutched to her chest.

'Here you are.'

Guy's voice behind her made Lucy jump and she spun round, her heart jerking madly, although whether from the shock or the sight of him she couldn't tell. Just by standing there in the doorway, he managed to charge the hushed, exclusive atmosphere with energy so that the very air seemed to be vibrating with his presence.

'It's you,' she said faintly.

'It *is* my office,' he pointed out, the blue, blue eyes glinting with amusement.

And he was probably wondering what a lowly receptionist was doing there gaping at the view. 'Er…Sheila asked me to print this out for you,' said Lucy, hastily laying the file on the desk. 'Her father's in hospital so she's had to go and see him. She gave me her password and told me where I would find the files.'

'Yes, she said she'd spoken to you. She managed to get hold of me on my mobile in the end, but it sounds as if she'll have to be in Wales for a few days at least.'

Guy picked up the file and flicked through it. He was wearing a classic charcoal-grey suit and she found herself watching his hands. They were strong and capable-looking, with deft fingers and very clean nails, and the memory of them holding that lasso made Lucy suddenly giddy.

She shouldn't have skipped breakfast.

'Thank you for doing this.' The blue eyes held an arrested expression as he looked up from the papers. 'This is exactly what I needed.'

'I just did what Sheila told me to do.'

'She explained what she'd asked you to do, but I can't say I expected you to have it done quite so soon.'

'I've sent those emails she mentioned, too,' said Lucy, 'but it's too early to contact the caterers about the reception this evening. I'll do that later.'

She glanced at her watch. 'There should be someone in Human Resources now. Sheila suggested contacting them for some temporary cover while she's away. Would you like me to do that for you, or will you ring them yourself?'

'Why can't you do it?' said Guy, dropping the file back onto his desk.

'Me?'

'Why not? You can obviously use a computer.'

'Well, yes, but—'

'And you can answer a phone.'

'Yes, of course, but I—'

'And you've got common sense—although that's not always obvious, I must admit,' he added with one of his glinting looks. 'Most important of all, you're here and you know Sheila's password, which means you can start straight away and I don't need to wait for HR to shunt people around or get someone from an agency. That makes you the best candidate in my book.'

Lucy swallowed. 'I'm not qualified to be a PA at this level.'

'That doesn't mean you can't do it,' said Guy.

'But I've never done a job like that before!' Lucy couldn't believe how casually he seemed to be taking it all. Wasn't he worried that she would come in and make a huge mess of everything?

'Well, here's your chance to try,' he said, and then he fixed her with keen blue eyes. 'Or are you scared that you won't be able to do it?'

That brought her chin up immediately. 'I'm not scared.'

'Good, because you shouldn't be,' said Guy. Perching on the edge of his desk, he put his hands in his pockets and regarded Lucy thoughtfully. 'I think you're capable of a lot more than you think you are, Cinders,' he said, not ungently.

'I don't know...' Lucy chewed her lip anxiously. She might not be scared, but that didn't mean she wasn't nervous. Very. 'I suppose I do avoid situations where I might be asked to do something I don't know how to do. Perhaps it's something to do with being the baby of the family. There's always someone to look after you, and so nobody has very high expectations of you.'

'Or is that you don't have very high expectations of yourself?' said Guy. 'I'm the youngest, too, and I know what it's like. I spent a lot of time drifting around, not wanting to do anything but have a good time, believing that was all I was good for.

'I don't regret those years at all,' he told her, 'and there's nothing wrong with having a good time, but...there was something missing. I was always looking for something else, some new thrill. I'd set myself physical challenges, and it never occurred to me that running a business could be far harder and just as stimulating. I only discovered what I could do when I came home and had to take over at Dangerfield & Dunn.'

'I don't think I'm ready to tackle being chairman just yet,' said Lucy nervously, and Guy laughed.

'Once you know what you can do as a PA, who knows where you'll end up?'

Lucy drew a deep breath. 'Well, all right, I'll do it, if you're sure. I'd better let Imogen know, though. I said I'd just be ten minutes. She'll be wondering what on earth I've been doing up here.'

Guy straightened and went round to sit at his desk. He pulled the file towards him as Lucy left to phone from Sheila's office. 'Tell her that you've been raising your expectations.'

In spite of her nervousness, Lucy couldn't help being excited at the prospect of taking over from Sheila for a while. Guy seemed to think that she could do it, so maybe she could. All she needed to do was keep her cool and put the memory of that kiss right out of her mind. From now on, he would be her boss. Not her pretend fiancé, not the boy who had once wanted to be a rodeo rider, not Bridget's son doing his best to live up to his father's expectations.

Not the man who had kissed her until her bones dissolved. Just her boss.

She could do that, Lucy told herself. No problem.

There had been days Lucy thought were busy down in Reception, but she had never worked as hard as she did that day. The phone rang constantly, emails banked up in Sheila's in-box, and there was a steady stream of people wanting to see Guy. He had one meeting after another, and Lucy had to make sure that he had all the right information to hand for each one. She supplied people with coffee when required and hurried back to Sheila's desk to set up new meetings, keep a careful eye on Guy's diary or check up on the arrangements for the reception Dangerfield & Dunn were hosting that night.

It was an eye-opening day for Lucy. She hadn't realised that she was capable of working that hard, or that she could cope with the avalanche of phone calls and emails and the multiple crises which all had to be dealt with immediately, without descending into panic or asking for help.

She saw a new side to Guy, too. He might look the same, he might smile the same smile, but this was not just the lazily good-humoured Guy who had somehow become so familiar to her. This Guy knew exactly what he was doing. He might wear a beautiful cashmere suit and sit in a luxurious office but there was nothing soft about the way he did business. Lucy could hear an edge of steel in his voice, and beneath the smile and the charm was a toughness she had only glimpsed before.

It made her feel funny inside whenever she thought about it.

'Are you still here?'

It was almost half past six when Guy came back from a meeting to find Lucy printing out one last document.

Her heart gave a little lurch at the sight of him, which was annoying as she had managed to keep it pretty steady for most of the day. She had been too busy to remember how it felt to kiss him, but now the memory was back with a vengeance and she was suddenly, acutely, aware that the floor was empty except for the two of them.

She kept her eyes on the printer, lifting out the document as soon as it was complete and putting it into its file. 'I'm just finishing now,' she said, glad she had something to keep her hands and eyes busy. Filing might not be glamorous, but it was a lot more dignified than flinging herself into his arms and begging him to kiss her again.

'I was wondering if I should just check that everything is

OK for the reception downstairs,' she went on, rather pleased at the coolness of her voice. 'It's starting soon.'

'I know,' said Guy. 'That's why I've come back. I'm supposed to be making a speech of welcome.'

Lucy nodded. 'I've put the notes for your speech on your desk.'

She went back to fretting about the reception, which had been occupying her all day and was a lot safer than noticing how well Guy's jacket fitted his broad shoulders, or wondering what it was about the line of his jaw that tangled her entrails into knots. 'I could just put my head round the door and see that there are no problems behind the scenes,' she said, talking to herself as much as to him. 'The guest list has been changing all day.'

'I've got a better idea,' said Guy, strolling over to prop himself against her desk. 'There's no need for you to skulk around behind the scenes. Why don't you come to the reception as a member of staff? You could probably do with a drink, couldn't you?'

Lucy was gasping for one, but it didn't seem very professional to admit it. 'I probably need something to eat more,' she said. 'I didn't have time for lunch.'

'No lunch! Poor Lucy. That never happened at Wirrindago, did it?' Guy's eyes rested on her face. 'I tell you what,' he said. 'We'll go to the reception, have a drink and some of those nice canapés that Sheila always organises. I'll make my speech and then I'll take you out to dinner to thank you for all your hard work today. You've been brilliant.'

'I'm not really dressed for a reception,' she prevaricated.

'Sure you are,' said Guy briskly. 'Everyone will be coming straight from work so they'll all be in office clothes.'

'They won't be in borrowed suits!'

'You look fine,' he soothed. He studied her scoop-necked

top and the neat little skirt whose matching jacket hung over the back of her chair. 'More than fine, in fact. Go and put your lipstick on, or whatever it is you women do before you go out, and we'll go.'

So Lucy found herself in his private bathroom, pulling the clip out of her hair with hands that weren't nearly as steady as she wanted. She looked a mess. Bending at the waist, she brushed her hair out vigorously before shaking it back and clipping it firmly away from her face once more. She was still at work after all. Executive PAs didn't let their hair tumble to their shoulders, and she had better not forget that a PA was all she was—and a temporary one at that.

Lipstick, blusher, a squirt of perfume and she was ready, but she found herself pausing with her hand on the bathroom door and taking a couple of deep steadying breaths before she put on a bright smile and went out to meet Guy.

The reception was held on the mezzanine floor, overlooking the dramatic semicircular atrium with its curved glass walls. In spite of what Guy had said about all the guests being in their office clothes, everyone seemed alarmingly well-dressed to Lucy. Until then, this suit of Meg's had been one of her favourites, and she had worn it several times, but now it was suddenly obvious that it came from a cheap and cheerful chain store.

Still, she might as well wear it with pride, Lucy decided. She was lucky she had a suit to wear at all. If she had to stick to her own wardrobe, she would be standing here in a T-shirt and jeans.

At least the reception was going well. The mezzanine was soon crowded and everyone who was supposed to come appeared. The buzz of chatter and laughter reverberated up into the stupendously high ceiling while the lights glittered in the mirrored glass.

Guy made a mercifully short but very funny speech that

had everyone laughing, and Lucy was conscious of a little thrill of pride as she watched him. She knew that he had given his speech some thought, but he didn't use notes and looked utterly relaxed as he stood up there and held the attention of all with the skill of a born performer.

Looking at him, she was conscious of a strange hollow feeling. With one part of her mind she registered the financier in the suit, the pale blue shirt with the faintest of stripes and the tie that matched perfectly, but with the other she saw him on the back of that horse, sitting easily in the saddle as he cantered around the ring, testing the weight of the rope in his hand, getting ready to send it uncoiling through the air.

How did the other guests see him? she wondered, glancing around her. They no doubt saw, as she had not seen at first, that he was a man with power, a man who could make hard decisions, a man who could laugh and still earn respect. They might see him as a successful financier, perhaps just as a vibrant, handsome man, even a charming and extraordinarily eligible bachelor, but did they know that he could lasso a calf? Could they guess how he bantered with the waiters in a small Italian restaurant, or the good-humoured way he accepted his mother's grumbling about his car?

Did they know that his lips were warm and his touch was sure and that the mere thought of kissing him was enough to liquefy her bones and send the blood to her head in a dizzying rush that left her shaken and hollow with the longing to kiss him again?

She did, and the knowing made her giddy all over again.

'Are you OK?' Guy had materialised at her side and was peering at her expression with concern.

'Yes, I'm just a bit…light-headed,' said Lucy truthfully. She gestured with her glass. 'The result of two glasses of champagne on an empty stomach, I suspect.'

And the thought of you—kissing you, touching you, holding you.

'Come on, you need feeding,' said Guy and took her arm, and even that was enough to make her pulse go into overdrive. 'I've done my bit here. Let's go.'

CHAPTER EIGHT

THEY walked down the steps together to the waiting limousine, but when the chauffeur got out to open the door for her, Lucy's nerve abruptly deserted her. She couldn't sit in the dark intimacy of the car with Guy, not tonight. She was afraid of being alone with him, afraid of what she might say and what she might do.

'Actually, Guy, I…I think I'll just go home,' she said. 'I'm really tired.'

Guy looked at her closely. 'Are you sure?'

'Yes. Really.'

'I'll get Steve to take you, then,' said Guy, but Lucy was already backing away.

'I'll take the tube,' she said. 'It's not late. Honestly, I'll be fine.'

By the next morning, though, her panic seemed ridiculous. Queuing for a cappuccino on her way into work, Lucy told herself that she had just been silly and that it had to stop. She couldn't start getting into a spin every time Guy came near her. She was supposed to be acting as his PA, for heaven's sake! And after her initial nervousness, she had really enjoyed the previous day. Maybe there was something in Guy's idea of raising her expectations.

She had just been over-tired last night, Lucy decided. That little turn had been brought on by a combination of weariness and champagne, that was all. It wouldn't be like that today. From now on she would be coolness personified. She would be super professional and treat Guy as no more than her boss, which was all that he was.

Even if he had kissed her twice.

And she wasn't even going to *think* about him kissing her any more, Lucy told herself sternly. Hadn't she decided she was going to grow up and be more responsible? That meant not being thrown into a tizzy by a couple of little kisses that had only ever been intended to wind her up anyway. She should treat them as a joke, the way Guy obviously did.

Fortified by caffeine and having talked herself into a positive frame of mind, Lucy sailed into work. She waved at Imogen and the new receptionist and joined the press for the lifts. Childish it might be, but it gave her a little thrill to press the button for the top floor. It felt as if she were literally going up in the world.

Guy was out all morning. He wouldn't be in until lunchtime, he had said, and Lucy told herself that it was much better that way. At least it was an opportunity to catch up on the backlog from the frantic activity of the day before. She worked steadily and didn't think about how empty the office felt without him—at least not more than five or six times an hour. There were far fewer distractions without him hanging around, too. Having to lift her head every time she heard the ping of the lift doors opening, just in case he had decided to cancel one of his meetings and come back early, obviously didn't count.

In the event, Guy strolled back into the office just as Lucy had taken an enormous bite of her crayfish and roquette sandwich, and she promptly choked.

'Sorry,' she mumbled, her mouth full, and frantically tried to deal with the rogue piece of lettuce that was somehow stuck between her teeth. So much for cool and professional. 'I wasn't expecting you.'

'I told you I would be in at lunchtime,' he said, surprised.

'I know. I…just wasn't expecting you right then.' Feeling a fool, Lucy brushed crumbs from her front. 'I left a whole lot of messages on your desk.'

'Good.' Guy shrugged off his long cashmere coat and hung it up. 'I had several comments this morning from people at the reception last night. They were all impressed by how well it was organised.'

'That was all down to Sheila.'

'I know,' he said, 'but it needed you to see it through. I gather you dealt with a number of last-minute hassles.'

'Well, there's always something, isn't there?' said Lucy awkwardly, rather embarrassed by his praise. It seemed to her that the success of the reception was entirely due to Sheila. All she had done was chase up a few details.

Expecting Guy to head for his office, she picked up her sandwich, but now he was taking off his jacket and rolling up his sleeves as if he were planning to make himself at home right where he was. 'I spoke to Sheila this morning,' he told her. 'She thinks that she's sorted out some care for her father, so she's hoping to be back next week.'

Next week. 'Oh.' Lucy put down her sandwich again.

It didn't look as if her glorious career as a PA was going to last long. Lucy was surprised at how disappointed she felt. It was nothing to do with the fact that she wouldn't be working with Guy any more, of course. She had just been enjoying doing something a bit more challenging. 'Will I be able to go back to Reception?' she asked, thinking of the new girl who had been sitting beside Imogen that morning.

'If you want to, but I was hoping you'd consider another job.'

She looked at him curiously as he pulled out a chair and sat down on the other side of her desk. 'What sort of job?'

'I want someone to arrange a party,' said Guy, 'and you seem like someone who could do that.'

'A party?' Lucy brightened. 'That sounds fun.'

'Not an ordinary party,' he warned her. 'It's being held to raise funds for a new paediatric unit in Michael's memory, so it needs to be glitzy and glamorous and spectacular and anything else that will persuade people to buy tickets at vastly inflated prices and create an atmosphere that will make them want to donate even more when they get there.'

Glitzy and glamorous. It was sounding better and better. She pulled a notebook towards her and looked for a pen. 'When do you want to have it?'

'That's the trouble. The venue is booked for a month's time.'

Lucy had just located a pen under the sandwich bag, but she froze at that. 'A *month?* That isn't long to arrange a glitzy party,' she said doubtfully. 'You have to book everything about a year in advance for big events.'

'We did start last year, but it's one of those things that's been dogged by ill luck, for some reason. The first organiser got pregnant and had to leave because of high blood pressure, her replacement only lasted a couple of weeks before accepting another job, and the next person picked up typhoid on holiday. There was someone in between but I can't honestly remember what happened to them,' he said.

'All I know is that the whole thing is a mess at the moment and if it doesn't get sorted we're going to have to cancel, which would be a pity. I need someone who can go in and work out what's been done and what needs to be done to make sure the event is a huge success—and then do it!

'I know it's short notice now, but anything can be done if you throw enough money at the problem. Sheila hasn't got time to sort it out, and the party really needs a touch of flair to rescue it...so we thought of you.' He fixed Lucy with his blue eyes. 'Are you up for it?'

'Is this another challenge?' she asked him.

Guy smiled. 'This would be a real one,' he said, 'but I know you could do it.'

Organising a party...how hard could it be? It might be hard work, but it would be fun. Lucy's eyes shone with sudden excitement. 'I'll have a go.'

'Excellent.' Guy got to his feet and retrieved his jacket from the back of the chair. 'That's settled, then. You can look at the files tomorrow, and start work properly as soon as Sheila gets back.'

Lucy was so excited at the prospect that she couldn't wait to get into work the next morning. Leaving early, she bounced into the kitchen to find Meg by the fridge, drinking orange juice out of the carton. Meg narrowed her eyes suspiciously at Lucy's bright-eyed expression.

'Who are you, and what have you done with my friend Lucy?' she asked sourly. 'You've taken her over and turned her into a workaholic with a career in the City.'

Lucy laughed as she buttoned up her jacket and swung her bag over her shoulder. 'It's only for a month, Meg. It's hardly a career.'

Still, she couldn't help but think of the possibilities that could open up in the future. Lucy hung on to the rail as the tube train rocked and swayed through the long tunnels. If she made a success of this party, she could find other jobs in events management. It was the perfect career for her—fun, focused, short-term. She couldn't believe that she hadn't thought of it before.

Smiling, she swung up the steps and through the doors into Dangerfield & Dunn. 'Hi!' she called gaily to Imogen, who was absorbed in reading something below the desk.

Imogen's head jerked up and her eyes widened. 'Lucy…hi,' she said, hurriedly closing the paper she had been reading.

Funny, thought Lucy as she joined the crowd waiting for the lifts. Imogen had looked at her in a very strange way.

It was the same in the lift. Lucy had the weirdest feeling that everyone was looking at her, but whenever she glanced back their eyes would slide away and they would stare studiously at the lights above the doors.

Odd. Did she have her skirt caught in her knickers or something? As discreetly as she could, Lucy felt round the back of her legs, but everything seemed to be in place. Her hair was clipped up as usual and her shoes matched, and she didn't *think* she had anything on her face.

Oh, well. There wasn't much she could do about it until she could get to a mirror, and Lucy was feeling too positive to waste too much time feeling embarrassed until she needed to. She practically bounced out of the lift and swung down to Sheila's office, throwing her jacket over the chair and switching on the computer in one energetic movement.

'Ah, Lucy.'

She spun round to see Guy, lounging in the doorway to his office, and right on cue her pulse went into overdrive. Everything about him seemed to be so sharply defined, so immediate, that the very air seemed to crackle around him.

'Hi,' she said as casually as she could. 'I wasn't expecting you in yet.'

'Something came up.' There was a peculiar note in his voice that made Lucy look at him sharply, reminded for some reason of the strange looks she had been getting that morning.

'Have I got a smudge on my nose or something? Everyone keeps staring at me.'

Guy straightened from the door and she noticed for the first time that he had a newspaper in his hand. 'You're behind with the news, Lucy. I take it you haven't seen this yet?'

'Er, no...' Oh, God, had there been some disaster she ought to know about? She should probably care now about things like the Dow Jones Index and the strength of the pound. As it was, she had picked up a free paper on her way into the tube, but she had been too busy daydreaming about her new career in events management to read it.

'In that case, you might like to read this.' Guy handed her the paper, which had been folded back to the gossip column.

Lucy took it obediently and stared down at it, wondering why she was supposed to care if one of the princes had been to a party. It didn't seem like very exciting news to her.

'Not there,' said Guy, seeing what she was reading. 'Take a look at the next paragraph.'

Humouring him, Lucy began to read out loud. '"*I understand that another eligible bachelor is soon to be off the market,*"' she read. '"*There will be a lot of disappointed socialites out there this morning. Guy Dangerfield, whose name has been linked with some of London's most beautiful women, including Cassandra Wolfe, has turned his back on the party circuit to marry his PA, Lucy We...*"'

Lucy's voice, which had been getting slower and slower as she realised where the article was going petered out at last. 'Oh...my....God!'

'Quite,' said Guy.

Aghast, Lucy raised her eyes from the paper and stared at Guy. 'How did they get hold of this?'

'I was hoping you might be able to tell me that,' he said. 'I certainly haven't told anyone.'

'Nor have I. Only the Pollards know.' Her face darkened. 'Unless that nurse of Richard's said something.'

Guy frowned. 'How would a nurse know that we were engaged?'

'Well, she was there when Frank told Ellen and Richard about you so she might have overheard. It's not my fault,' she protested defensively as exasperation crossed his face, and then she stopped. 'Yes, it *is* my fault,' she said in a different tone. 'If I hadn't said anything to Frank, this would never have happened.'

She looked back down at the paper, skimming through the rest of the piece with increasing disbelief. '"…insepar-able…Guy barely left her side at a reception…left together…a definite chemistry…" What?' she interrupted herself, outraged. 'What *is* all this stuff?' she demanded. 'And where did they get it from? Richard's nurse wasn't there last night!'

'I suppose, once the idea had been suggested, some jour-nalist started sniffing around.' Guy shrugged. 'It wouldn't be too difficult to find someone who was at the reception last night and then ask if they'd noticed you—as I'm sure everyone did.'

'But why?' Lucy was still fuming. What did they mean, "a definite chemistry"? 'I didn't do anything. I wasn't trying to draw attention to myself. I just stood there and drank a couple of glasses of champagne. Why would anyone notice that?'

'You're the kind of girl who gets noticed,' said Guy.

There was an odd note in his voice and she looked at him sharply, suspecting mockery, but when her eyes met his the teasing laughter she was expecting to see was entirely absent and she could read nothing in the blue depths.

Nothing that she recognised, anyway, but her heart was suddenly thudding and the air leaking out of her lungs until she made herself look away. She threw the paper on to her desk.

'That's such rubbish,' she said, not quite as firmly as she would have liked. 'It makes it sound as if you…as if we…'

'Are in love?' Guy suggested as she trailed off, a little uncertain.

'Well, yes…which we're not, *obviously*,' said Lucy, hoping that she sounded more convincing to him than she did to herself. 'They've just made it all up.'

'I know, but someone must have told them about us leaving together,' he pointed out. 'One tiny snippet of truth makes it harder to deny the whole story.' He leant against Sheila's desk and rubbed his jaw as he thought. 'I think it's probably best to ignore it,' he decided after a while.

Lucy looked dubious. 'What if anyone asks about it?'

'Just say no comment,' he said. 'They'll soon lose interest. There'll be something or someone else to talk about tomorrow.'

'That's all very well if a journalist rings up, but what about everyone else?' she asked. 'I can't say *no comment* if Imogen rings up and asks why I didn't tell her that we were having a relationship.'

'Why would she do that?'

'I would in her position,' said Lucy. 'No wonder she gave me that funny look this morning! She was great to me and we got to be good friends, and now all she'll think is that I lied to her. And what about Sheila?' It was getting worse the more she thought about it. 'How's *she* going to feel when she reads that I'm apparently your new PA? It'll seem like I've walked off with her boss *and* her job!'

Guy sighed. 'I'll call Sheila and explain, and I suppose I'd better ring my mother, too, or there'll be all hell to pay, but we can't tell everyone the truth. That would just turn it into a bigger story. They'll go back to whoever contacted them at first and start poking around and, before you know where you are, they'll be asking why we would have lied to Frank Pollard in the first place.'

'So we do nothing?'

'I think it might be easier in the long run,' he decided. 'Let everyone think that we are having a relationship, but don't confirm the engagement. You told the Pollards that we didn't want to go public until Meredith gets back, so we'll stick with that as an excuse for no announcement.'

'That explains why we haven't told anyone we're engaged,' said Lucy, 'but it doesn't explain why we haven't told anyone we're having a relationship in the first place.'

'No one's going to expect details, are they?'

'Of course they are!' Lucy stared at him in disbelief. 'No woman would smile politely when she heard about a secret engagement and then not ask any more. *Oh, so you're not announcing your engagement yet? OK. Nice weather, isn't it?* No, she's going to want to know how we met, when the relationship started, and why I didn't tell anyone about it—and that's just for starters. She'll be asking how our relationship works, whose idea it was to get married, when the wedding is, what dress I'm wearing and how many bridesmaids I'd like.'

Guy was looking appalled. 'Can't you just tell them to mind their own business?'

She just shook her head. 'That's not how women work.'

'Well, I'm not going into any of that stuff,' he said firmly. 'I'll admit that we're having a relationship and that we're going to get married, and I'll say that we're not making our engagement public for now, but that's it. I'm not saying any more than that.'

Lucy looked sceptical. 'If you can get away with it…but I don't see how you can, unless you only talk to men for the next few days. Which, come to think of it, probably isn't that hard when you're an investment banker.' She dropped into the chair as the implications of the article began to hit her properly. 'What about your merger?' she asked, and Guy sighed again.

'I'll just have to hope that Bill Sheldon doesn't read the gossip columns.'

The words were barely out of his mouth before the phone on Sheila's desk rang. Taking a calming breath, Lucy answered it, listened and then put the call on hold. She looked at Guy. 'Would you believe me if I told you it was Bill Sheldon for you?'

'You're joking?'

Lucy shook her head. 'Uh-uh.'

'Oh, God.' Guy's eyes rolled up towards the ceiling, but he had little choice than to take the phone from her.

'Bill, how are you?' he asked, his cheerfulness sounding forced for once. '...Oh, you did? Yes, yes it is a bit unexpected... No, we haven't known each other long...it's all happened rather suddenly...'

A muscle was twitching in his jaw by the time he cut the connection and handed the phone back to Lucy.

'That was Bill,' he said unnecessarily. 'Calling to offer me his congratulations,' he added, tight-lipped, 'and obviously to find out why I hadn't thought about mentioning you before.'

'Couldn't you just tell him to mind his own business?' asked Lucy sweetly, quoting his own suggestion back at him, and had the satisfaction of provoking Guy into a glare.

'He suggested that I take you along to some party he's hosting with his daughter next Friday,' he said thinly, 'and when Bill Sheldon makes a suggestion like that in the middle of merger negotiations, it's as well to agree that it sounds like a fine idea. So if you had any other plans for that Friday night, you can remake them!'

Lucy bridled. 'Why does he want to meet me?'

'He wants to know if I'm the man he thought I was,' said Guy. 'He's got reason now to think I'm keeping something back. If I'm secretive about you, he's thinking, what else am I hiding? So we'll go, and convince Bill and everyone else who needs to know that what we have here is a whirlwind love affair and nothing else.'

Shaking his head, he turned towards his office. 'My life was simple until I met you, Lucy!'

'Sorry,' she said in a small voice.

'Well, we're committed now,' he said, resigned, 'so we'll just have to go with it, and in the meantime let's try and do some work here.'

'Right,' said Lucy, swinging her chair round to face the computer. 'Right.'

But it was hard to get much done when the phone rang off the hook. Friends, business colleagues, reporters... Was she the only person in London who hadn't read the piece in the paper that morning? And, of course, they all wanted to know if she was Guy's fiancée and PA, Lucy. It was easiest just to deny it and pretend that Lucy was unavailable, although obviously this didn't work when Meg called.

'I know you're a body snatcher and are holding Lucy against her will,' she said. 'All that going to work early was a dead giveaway, but now I'm sure that you're an alien, because my friend Lucy would *never* even think of getting engaged without telling me!'

It took Lucy some time to coax Meg out of her crossness. 'It's a long story,' she said, deciding that she owed Meg the truth. She didn't care what Guy said about not telling anyone else. 'I'll tell you all about it tonight, I promise you.'

The more the phone rang, the more Lucy realised quite what an awkward position she had put Guy in. She had had no idea that one tiny snippet of gossip could cause such a furore, and it was hard not to feel guilty about the way her careless comment to Frank had snowballed out of hand.

Still, things could have been worse, she tried to reassure herself. The story about their engagement might not be true, but it wasn't as if it would hurt anyone. Neither of them was involved with anyone else, after all, and the interest wouldn't last for ever. Sheila would come back, she would organise the fund-raising party and when that was over…

Yes, what then, Lucy? a little voice inside her enquired.

Well, then she would leave. Appalled by the way her heart sank at the very thought of leaving, Lucy pulled herself together. Leaving had always been part of the plan. She had obligations in Australia, a promise to Hal which she needed to fulfil. After that, she could decide what she wanted to do. She could get herself another job, a proper job, even.

And no doubt Guy would be relieved to have her out of his hair. He would marry eventually—someone glamorous and responsible, to make Bridget happy—and Lucy would become nothing more than a funny story he would tell at dinner parties.

She could just see him, leaning back in his chair, ready to entertain everyone. The blue eyes would be dancing. 'I once had a PA with a rich fantasy life,' he would begin, and he would have that undercurrent of laughter in his voice, the one that made her want to laugh even if he were only talking about a tax return. 'Talk about a dizzy blonde! At one point she actually pretended that I had asked her to marry me.'

Guy would tell the story well, of course. He would tell it against himself, with that self-deprecating irony that was so typical of him. How all the other guests would laugh to hear how Lucy had embroiled him in her problems!

The image was so vivid that Lucy pushed her chair abruptly away from the desk and stood up. That was quite enough thinking. She didn't want to think about leaving, Guy, chemistry, this stupid engagement or anything else.

She would think about the party instead, Lucy decided. Now Sheila's office was under control, she could go and get the files and make a start. She might even stay late tonight. It sounded as if there was a lot of work to be done in sorting everything out, and besides, she thought, it would be a good excuse to avoid everyone else going home at the same time. She could sneak out when the building was quiet. She didn't care if it was cowardly.

Unfortunately, her careful plan to keep a low profile was foiled by George Duncan, Director of Human Resources, who came along, all smiles, a little while later and asked if he could have a quick word with Guy—and with her.

'It's about your engagement,' he explained when they were all settled on the sofas in Guy's office. 'Of course, we know that you don't want to make an official announcement yet, but the staff are all so pleased for you and everyone has been asking if we could mark the occasion in some way.'

He beamed from one to the other and Lucy just hoped that her sinking heart didn't show in her expression as she forced a smile in return. Guy, she noticed with a touch of resentment, was looking cucumber cool.

'We'd very much like to offer you our congratulations,' George was saying, 'and we wondered if you would both join us all for a glass of champagne at six o'clock. Just a small in-house celebration on the mezzanine,' he added a little anxiously, perhaps picking up on the tension in the atmosphere after all.

Lucy was sitting next to Guy and he put his hand over hers on the sofa. 'That's very kind, George,' he said smoothly. 'Lucy and I would love to come, wouldn't we, darling?'

Burningly conscious of his hand over hers, Lucy made her smile widen. 'Of course,' she said. 'It's a lovely idea.'

'Splendid!' Reassured, George hauled himself to his feet. 'We'll see you at six, then.'

'What have we done?' Lucy muttered to Guy as they waited for the lift to take them down to the mezzanine.

'*We?* What have *we* done?' Guy raised his brows incredulously. 'Shouldn't that be what have *I* done?'

'Listen, it wasn't me barely leaving my side at the reception last night,' she snapped. 'And what happened to your theory about people losing interest in the situation if we just ignored it?'

'I didn't say it would happen today,' Guy pointed out.

'What if it never happens? This is awful,' said Lucy fretfully. 'It feels as if everything is snowballing out of control. Now there's this party, and everyone's going to be so pleased for us when we're *lying* to them. It's all wrong.'

'Perhaps you'll think about that next time you start inventing fiancés' said Guy with a meaningful look. He pointed a finger at her. 'No more stories,' he told her. 'Let's just stick with the one we've got.

'Look, I don't feel comfortable lying to my staff either,' he went on when Lucy looked dubious. 'I've never done it before, and I hope never to have to do it again, but they'll feel foolish if we tell them the engagement isn't real after they've gone to so much trouble. So we're going to have to put on a happy face, smile and say thank you, and do our best to ensure that not one of the people on the mezzanine tonight even suspects that they've taken part in a farce.'

Guy had already pushed the button to call the lift, but Lucy reached out impatiently and pushed it again, twice for good measure. 'They're going to know sooner or later when it becomes clear that we are not, in fact, getting married.'

'Not necessarily. Nobody needs to know that our engagement wasn't real,' he pointed out. 'Lots of people get engaged and never get round to getting married. When all the interest has died down, we can just let it be known that we've changed our minds.'

'Or we could have a big argument,' Lucy suggested.

'Exactly,' said Guy, nodding agreement. His eyes glinted down at her. 'I'll realise eventually that you're totally unreasonable and call the whole thing off.'

'Why can't I be the one to call it off?' she demanded, getting into the spirit of the thing.

He feigned shock. 'What possible reason could you have for not wanting to marry me?'

'Oh, I'm sure I'll think of something,' said Lucy airily. 'I'll hint darkly about the kind of things you like to get up to when we're on our own.'

Guy grinned. 'That'll make me sound exciting!'

'Well, then, perhaps I'll just imply that the magic has gone,' she improvised. 'Or I'll say that I've fallen in love with someone else.'

Even as she said it, she realised how unconvincing it was going to sound. How likely was it that she would fall in love with someone else if she had Guy? She would never be able to carry it off.

'Or,' said Guy, 'you could tell the truth.'

'The truth?' She looked at him blankly and the corner of his mouth twitched.

'I realise it would be a novel experience for you, Cinders! Just say that you're going back to Australia to be with Kevin.'

Kevin. She had almost forgotten what he looked like. Lucy's eyes slid away from Guy's as the lift arrived with a ping and the doors slid open.

'Yes, I could say that, I suppose.'

'But not too soon,' he warned, standing back to let her into the lift before him. 'Wait until after the party next month. That would be a good time for you to leave anyway,' he added. 'If we break off our engagement before then, people are going to feel awkward and wonder what they should be saying. Once you're not around any more, it'll be easier for them to feel sorry for me.'

As if anyone was ever going to feel sorry for Guy.

It made sense, Lucy had to admit. She didn't want to be trapped in this embarrassing pretence any longer than she had to be and, once the party was over, she would have no reason to stay any longer.

So why was the thought of leaving settling inside her like a cold stone settling inside her?

'Smile,' said Guy under his breath as the lift stopped. 'Remember how much in love we are!'

CHAPTER NINE

THE mezzanine was almost as crowded as it had been for the reception the night before. Lucy couldn't believe how many people were waiting for them, each of them choosing to stay after work and wish them well rather than go home.

Her throat felt tight, but she found a smile, although she nearly lost it again when a great cheer went up as they spotted Guy. He was looking as lazily good-humoured as ever, and he grinned down at her as he took hold of her hand. His fingers were warm and reassuring, and she found herself blushing exactly as if she were going to be a real bride.

They were barely out of the lift before they were engulfed by well-wishers. Lucy had never been kissed so much before. She was soon separated from Guy, and she missed his hand around hers. Whenever she looked for him, he was there, smiling, laughing, effortlessly the warm, vibrant centre of the room.

He made it look so easy, she thought. She knew that everyone who spoke to him had the sense that Guy had really noticed them, that he was pleased to see them and appreciated that they had taken the trouble to come. Once their eyes met through the crowd and he mouthed 'all right?' and Lucy felt instantly steadied. Smiling, she nodded and turned away to find herself face to face with Imogen.

'Well?' demanded Imogen, putting her hands on her hips.

Lucy couldn't help laughing at her mock-threatening stance. 'I know, I know! I would have told you, Imogen, but I didn't know how I felt about Guy myself for ages.'

'I did.'

'You did what?' Lucy asked, puzzled.

'I knew there was something between you and Guy straight away.'

'You *did?*'

Imogen rolled her eyes. 'It was obvious, Lucy! I could tell by the way you looked at each other, and by the way you *didn't* look at each other. Either way, there was always a kind of sizzle in the air between you. I used to get quite hot just watching you,' she told Lucy, who belatedly tried to smooth her expression. It probably wasn't a good idea to boggle at Imogen as if she were astounded at the news that she and Guy had seemed attracted to each other. A real fiancée would have picked up the vibes herself. 'I wasn't at all surprised when I saw that piece in the paper,' Imogen finished, 'although I do think you might have told me!'

It seemed that Imogen was not the only one who claimed to have known all along that she and Guy were in love. Lucy began to feel quite uneasy. How could it have been so obvious to everyone when it wasn't true?

Unless it was true.

Lucy's blue gaze found Guy on the other side of the room. He was being hugged by a group of cleaners, who were all shrieking with laughter as he teased them. He wasn't looking at her, but she could still feel the warmth of his smile lighting up the room.

The world seemed to judder to an abrupt halt, leaving Lucy jarred and breathless.

Oh, God, it *was* true. Of course it was true. Of *course* she was in love with him. What a fool she had been! Lucy berated herself. Imogen was right. It had been obvious. The only one who hadn't seen it until now was her.

And Guy, she hoped.

Guy… Lucy smiled and chatted and did her best to seem like any other radiant fiancée, but inside she was reeling. When had it happened? When had he become the very centre of her existence? When had his presence, the smile in his eyes and the touch of his hands and the turn of his head, become as necessary to her as breathing?

Sipping her champagne, Lucy was feeling a little sick. It was as if everything that she had believed true about herself had been swished away, leaving her hollow and slightly giddy.

Guy. How long had she wanted him? Needed him? Loved him?

It wasn't just the way he looked, it was the man he was, Lucy thought. A man who was so much more than she had realised when she had dismissed him so casually in Australia. She knew him better now. She knew how patient he was with his mother, how generous to his staff. He was a man tough in negotiations, kind to cleaners, friendly to waiters, charming to all. No wonder everyone loved him.

They didn't love him the way she did. But how could she tell Guy that? Only a few weeks ago, she had been insisting that she loved Kevin. He would never believe her if she confessed how she felt now—and why should he? He knew that she had spent her whole life tumbling from one enthusiasm to another. Of course he would assume that loving him was just another passing infatuation for her.

It wasn't, though. Lucy knew that, deep in her core—a part of herself she hadn't even known existed before. Always before, she had tumbled joyfully into imagining herself in love, but this time it was different. This time she was almost scared by the intensity of the feeling. This time she had to see past the romance of falling in love with someone wonderful to some hard truths.

First of which was the fact that Guy wasn't in love with her.

And why should he be, after all? All she had done for him was snipe at him, let him rescue her and then pitch him into an embarrassing situation that might yet jeopardise an important merger.

Lucy cringed inwardly when she thought of how casually she had treated Guy, how carelessly she had taken his help for granted. How could she ever hope that he would love her? She wasn't a serious person. She had never stuck at anything, had never made a success of anything. She had just drifted around, having a good time. Guy deserved more than that.

Maybe *she* deserved more than that, too.

What was it that Guy had said about having higher expectations of herself? He had changed, he had fulfilled his potential, and she could, too. He had offered her a chance with this new job, and that would be a start. So what if it was only temporary? After she had kept her promise to Hal, there was no reason why she shouldn't find a career of her own. No reason why she couldn't make something of herself, and prove to herself as much as to Guy that she was someone worth loving.

Someone was clinking a knife against a glass and gradually the hubbub in the room diminished in response. Lucy found herself pushed towards a dais where Guy was standing next to George. They were both looking for her and, as she emerged at the front of the crowd, Guy smiled in a way that made her heart stutter. He's playing a part, she reminded herself, taking the hand he held out and letting herself be drawn into the circle of his arm

She needed to play a part too, although hers was more difficult than his. Guy just had to pretend to be in love with her. She had to pretend that she was pretending, but be convincing at the same time. It was the least she could do after landing him in this mess. Guy had made it clear that no one here should guess that their engagement wasn't real, and she wouldn't let him down.

So Lucy smiled and let herself relax against Guy, sliding her arm around his waist. George embarked on a speech, but she hardly heard a word of it, too aware of Guy, of the lovely solid warmth of him beneath her hand, of the new terrifying knowledge of how much she wanted everyone else to vanish so that she could turn into him, hold him closer, press her lips above his collar and kiss her way up his throat. She wanted to burrow into his sureness and his strength, to lose herself in his touch and his taste…

There was a burst of clapping as George got to the end of his speech at last. Glasses were lifted to a chorus of 'Lucy and Guy' and then Guy was stepping forward to reply. Lucy was intensely grateful that she wasn't being called upon to string two words together. It was all she could do to keep her smile in place while her body jumped and twitched with the need to crawl all over him.

Guy had let go of her waist, but he kept a firm hold of her hand. Lucy let her fingers curl around his, hanging on to his reassuring warmth and steadiness, and tried to cool the fever humming in her blood.

'I want to thank you all for your good wishes and for being here this evening,' he said. 'I know Lucy is as touched as I am.' He glanced down at her and she nodded her agreement, even managing a smile when all she wanted to do was to shout, *Forget about them! Lay me down on the floor here and make love to me!*

'To be honest,' Guy went on with a disarming grin, 'realising that we want to spend our lives together has been almost as much of a surprise to us as it must have been to you. Tonight is the first time it has really seemed true, and that's thanks to you. Being together feels very new to both of us, but it feels right too, and it's wonderful to know that so many people are happy for us. Neither of us will forget this evening, will we, Lucy?'

'No.' She would certainly never forget, thought Lucy. She would never forget the moment when she'd realised how much she loved him.

'So thank you all, very much,' Guy finished, and there was another storm of applause, followed by a peculiarly expectant silence.

Still dazed by his nearness and her own desire, it took Lucy a moment to realise what they were all waiting for. When she did, her eyes met Guy's and her heart turned over. He knew what they wanted. The smile deepened in his eyes, spreading over his face as he bent his head towards her, and there was an almost audible sigh of release from everyone watching as his lips touched hers and he kissed her at last.

The touch of his mouth sent a jolt of response through Lucy. The earth seemed to shift beneath her feet and the hand that wasn't curled tightly around his came up instinctively to clutch at the lapel of his jacket and keep herself steady. It felt so good, so sweet, so *right* to be kissing him that she forgot that they were being watched by the entire staff of Dangerfield & Dunn and gave herself up to the sheer relief of being able to kiss him back.

Guy must have felt her yielding against him. His arm tightened around her and for a moment his kiss was hard and hungry. Lucy's body flared in response to its fierce insistence and she pressed closer, oblivious to the watching crowd, to anything but the feel of his lips on hers, the taste of his mouth, the strength of the arm encircling her.

To anything but the fact that he was Guy and she loved him and she was in his arms.

It felt so wonderful that when Guy made to break away she made an inarticulate murmur of protest and held on tighter, but if she had forgotten the others watching with avid interest, he clearly hadn't. One last hard kiss and he had lifted his head so that he could look down into her face. He was smiling but the blue eyes held an arrested expression and all Lucy could do was stare back at him, dizzy with wanting him.

The next moment he had looked away, still smiling, to lift a hand and acknowledge the cheers. How did he *do* that? Lucy wondered wildly. How could he seem so normal? *His* bones clearly hadn't dissolved, his head wasn't reeling, his body wasn't humming in angry protest at the abrupt end to that kiss.

Because it had just been a kiss to Guy, Lucy realised, slowly coming to her senses. Why would it be anything else? And right now he was probably wondering why she had been kissing him back so lovingly. There was pretending and there was pretending, he would be thinking. She could practically see his mind clicking, raising an internal eyebrow as he inevitably came up with the right conclusion. Guy might be a lot of things but a fool wasn't one of them, especially not where women were concerned.

Lucy didn't want Guy to know that she had fallen in love with him. She didn't want to see him withdraw slightly, to be embarrassed or to explain, very kindly, that he hadn't meant anything when he'd kissed her. She didn't need him to tell her that. To Guy, she had never been a serious person, and if you weren't a serious person, you didn't get treated seriously. Lucy could see that now.

Well, that was all going to change, and when it *had* changed they would see how he felt about kissing her then.

In the meantime, she needed to persuade him that she had simply been playing along in her role.

With an enormous effort, Lucy stiffened her legs and made herself move out of the safe circle of his arm, her smile bright as she waved and blushed the way a real fiancée would.

'Well, that didn't go too badly,' said Guy as he settled into the back of the limousine with a barely suppressed sigh of relief. They had finally managed to extricate themselves from the celebrations, which looked set to carry on without them, and Guy had insisted on giving Lucy a lift back to Meg's.

'What's everyone going to think if they see me hopping into my car while my fiancée plods off to the tube?' he had said when Lucy had tried to protest that it wasn't necessary.

It had been a long day and Lucy had to admit that she wasn't really in the mood for the long trek home. It was a relief just to be able to sink back into the luxurious leather and close her eyes against the aching awareness of Guy beside her, the planes of his face thrown into relief by each streetlamp that they passed.

'Are you OK?' he asked in concern.

Lucy forced a smile. 'I'm fine. A bit tired, that's all.'

'It's been quite a day, hasn't it?' Guy shook his head, half-smiling. 'I think we managed to brush through it all right, though. Everyone seems utterly convinced that we really are engaged.'

'It's amazing, isn't it?' she agreed, keeping her voice deliberately light. 'You should have been an actor.'

'You were good, too,' said Guy, and his eyes rested on her mouth. 'That kiss was really very convincing.'

'I wondered if I might have overdone it a bit,' said Lucy

as casually as she could, although her heart was thumping painfully with the memory. 'I wanted everyone to think that I was besotted by you.'

'You succeeded. You even had me convinced!'

'Maybe I should take up acting, too. That's a career I haven't tried.' Lucy gazed out of the window. It was funny how her mind could nod approvingly at her words while her body raged in furious denial. *Stop with all this pretending*, it seemed to be saying. *Just tell him how you feel, and then throw yourself into his arms. What are backseats and dark windows for?*

Lucy made herself ignore it. 'I do feel bad about deceiving everyone. They were all there for you tonight.'

'And for you,' said Guy. 'You've only been at the bank a matter of weeks and already everybody knows you. I watched you tonight, Cinders. You were brilliant. You seemed to be having such a good time. You've got a real ability to light up a room.'

No, that's you, she wanted to say. 'We're quite a team when we get going, aren't we?' she said lightly instead.

'Yes,' said Guy without taking his eyes from her face. 'I'm beginning to think we are.'

There was a short silence. It seemed to reverberate around the car, and Lucy ran her tongue over suddenly dry lips as her gaze skittered away from his. Leaning forward, she peered out of the window. 'The traffic's terrible,' she said, rather proud of how cool she sounded. 'Why don't I get out here and you can go straight home?'

'Certainly not,' said Guy. 'But it might be easier if you'd think about moving in with me for a while. It would look a lot more convincing if we were living together, and it would save a lot of travelling time whenever we go out.'

'I don't think that's a good idea,' said Lucy.

'You'd have your own room, of course.'

'It's not that.' Lucy didn't know how to tell him that living with him would be torture. How could she be with him every evening and not touch him, not tell him that she needed him, that she loved him? The only way that she was going to get through this was to keep some distance between them.

'I like living at Meg's,' she told him. 'I'd rather keep some privacy.'

'You're not worried that everyone will wonder why you're choosing to live with Meg rather than the man you love?'

Lucy could tell from his voice that he was amused. 'Perhaps they'll think that I'm saving myself for my wedding night,' she suggested, but Guy shook his head.

'They're not going to think that, Lucy.'

'Why not?'

'Because they only have to look at you to know that you're the kind of girl who does everything wholeheartedly. You're not a girl who stops and has a good think before she commits herself. You're not sensible and prudent and careful. When a girl like you falls in love, she does it completely. She doesn't sit at home and save herself.'

Lucy drew a breath and met his eyes squarely. 'Maybe I'm not a girl like that any more,' she said. 'Maybe I've changed.'

Meg looked at her as if she were mad when she tried to explain why she didn't want to move in with Guy. 'That alien really did a number on you, didn't it?'

Lucy had told her the truth about the supposed engagement, and had done her best to keep her feelings for Guy out of it, but, as she had feared, Meg had zoomed in on that straight away.

'I don't understand why you don't go and live with him,' she said. 'Come on, something's bound to happen if you're both there in the dark. Guy won't be able to keep his hands off you. If you ask me, he fancies the pants off you already.'

'I don't want him to fancy me.'

Meg stared at her. 'I thought you were in love with him.'

'I am, that's just the point. I want him to love me—*me*, not some pretty girl who happens to be conveniently in his flat.'

'Well, he will when he gets to know you.'

Lucy sighed. 'That's the trouble. I've started to wonder what there is to know. Am I just pretty, frivolous Lucy West, always up for a laugh, or is there more to me? And if there is, what is it? I think I need to find out, Meg,' she said, looking at her baffled friend. 'If I don't know who I am, how can Guy, and if he doesn't know me, how can he love me?'

'You haven't forgotten the Sheldons' party tonight, have you?'

Lucy jumped as Guy appeared at her office door, and her heart performed a set of spectacular gymnastics. She had spent the past week avoiding him as much as possible, and when she did have to speak to him about anything, she had been cool to the point of frostiness.

Desperate not to let him guess the depth of her new, scarily powerful, feelings for him, she had retreated behind a barrier of cool aloofness that had Guy amused at first, then obviously puzzled. It had been a relief when Sheila had returned and she could throw herself into organising the fund raiser. She was given her own office, which helped, and, although Lucy missed the charge of Guy's presence, it was easier not to have to spend the whole time clamping down on her feelings, or bracing herself against the urge to reach out for him and tell him she loved him.

It helped that the work was so interesting, too. She was excited by her plans for the party, and the fact that she only had three weeks to make it work added a burst of adrenalin. Lucy was determined for it to be a success. It felt as if this was her chance to prove something—to Guy and to herself.

'No, I haven't forgotten,' she said when her heart had stopped showing off and was accepting a rapturous round of applause. Breathe in, breathe out. See, she could do it. 'I've been worrying about what to wear.'

The invitation had said 'black tie'. 'Which means you go for glamour, big time,' Meg had said when consulted. They had been through Meg's entire wardrobe, but in the end nothing had been suitable and Lucy had blown half her salary that lunchtime on an outfit that she would never have dreamt of wearing even a month ago.

'I want to look like a grown-up,' she had told the girl in the shop, and she was now the proud possessor of her very first little black dress and the most glamorous shoes she had ever owned.

'I'm sure you'll look great,' said Guy. He paused, looking at her as if he wanted to say something else, but in the end he just told her that he would pick her up at eight.

'You look fab,' said Meg admiringly when Lucy came downstairs that night. 'Guy won't be able to keep his hands off you.'

The problem was likely to be the opposite, Lucy thought when Guy turned up in a dinner jacket. The most ordinary of men looked better in the austere black and white, and the effect on Guy, who was more handsome than he ought to be at the best of times, was devastating. The sight of him made Lucy's knees buckle and her stomach looped the loop crazily before it landed, panting and squirming helplessly, deep inside her.

Guy whistled when he saw her. 'You look all grown-up,' he said.

But, as soon as she walked into the party, Lucy's confidence in her appearance evaporated. The little black dress that she had been so pleased with, that had felt such an extravagance, suddenly seemed to have 'chain store' stamped all over it. Every other woman there was beautifully dressed, their tiniest accessories costing at least five times what Lucy had paid for her entire outfit.

It was like being in a parallel universe. It wasn't that the other guests weren't pleasant, but Lucy was used to parties where everyone was crammed into a narrow hallway or an even smaller kitchen, where the music was so loud that her ears buzzed for days afterwards, and she could barely see who she was talking to, let alone hear them.

At the Sheldons' party a string quartet played quietly in the background, discreet waiters circulated with trays of canapés and champagne, and the guests conversed in a civilised manner. There was no shouting, but no loud laughter either. Lucy felt Guy sigh beside her.

'Sometimes,' he said, 'I want to stand up on a chair and shout obscenities, just to see what everyone would do!'

It was such a relief to know that he found all the tastefulness a touch oppressive too that Lucy laughed. 'Or run away and jump in a fountain,' she suggested.

'Or dance on the table in a smoky bar.'

They smiled at each other, enjoying the images, enjoying each other's company as the constraint between them was forgotten for the moment.

'Tell me that the party for the paediatric unit isn't going to be like this,' said Guy.

'It isn't going to be like this,' said Lucy. 'It's going to be fun.'

'Promise?'

'I promise.'

Something indefinable changed in the air between them as their eyes met, and Guy put out a hand. 'Lucy—'

'Guy, how nice to see you!'

Startled, they both turned to see a dark, svelte woman, so beautifully groomed and so elegantly dressed that Lucy immediately felt crumpled.

'Saskia!' Guy kissed her cheek, then turned to introduce Lucy. 'This is Bill's daughter, Saskia Sheldon. Saskia, my fiancée, Lucy West.'

'I heard you were engaged,' said Saskia warmly. 'Congratulations! You must tell me all about it.'

Lucy let Guy do that, and watched the two of them as they talked. They made a good couple, she couldn't help thinking, both witty, intelligent, good-looking and charming. She really wanted to dislike Saskia, but she found herself admiring her instead and feeling deeply inadequate in comparison.

It was clear that Saskia was what Meredith would call a serious person. She was clever, attractive, successful, interesting and what was worse, she seemed genuinely nice. As Bill Sheldon's daughter, she evidently came from the same privileged background as Guy, but Lucy gathered from the conversation that she was a successful corporate lawyer in her own right.

Guy ought to be with a woman like Saskia, Lucy realised dully. She was surprised that he couldn't see it for himself. How could he look at her standing next to Saskia and not compare them? On the one hand, a mature, capable, beautiful woman, and, on the other, herself: scatty, cheaply dressed, unqualified, not a single accomplishment to her name. *You look all grown-up*, Guy had said and, although she had been pleased at the time, now she wondered if it meant that he normally thought of her as an adolescent, someone young and silly instead of the competent twenty-six-year-old she could be if she tried.

It was time she grew up.

The evening seemed endless. Lucy smiled brightly and chatted and longed for it to be over. It was a huge relief when Guy suggested they go.

'Are your shoes up for a walk?' he asked when they got outside. 'It's too nice an evening to go straight home, and I could do with a bit of air. Do you mind?'

They headed through Covent Garden and down Long Acre into Trafalgar Square, not touching, not talking much either, but Lucy was intensely conscious of Guy by her side, of his easy stride, of the familiar set of his shoulders and the hard, exciting angles of his face. The fuzzy light from streetlamps cast a protective blur over everything, hiding her expression, and her blood hummed with awareness and a kind of sadness. She couldn't imagine many more occasions when she would be alone with Guy like this.

'You're very quiet,' Guy said as they walked down the steps in front of the National Gallery. 'I know tonight wasn't much fun, but you did brilliantly. You charmed the pants off Bill Sheldon and his crusty old cronies. I was proud of you, even if you're not really my fiancée.'

'I felt horribly out of place,' Lucy confessed. The evening had been a depressing reminder of just how little she belonged in Guy's world.

'You didn't look it,' said Guy. 'You looked fantastic.' He stopped at the bottom of the steps and Lucy faltered to a halt as he turned to face her where she stood, a couple of steps above him so that their faces were on the same level. 'You still do,' he said.

His voice, very deep and very low, set Lucy's heart drumming painfully in her chest, and the look in his eyes made her pulse boom so thunderously that she could barely hear. Trafalgar Square was thronging with people, even at this time of night, and there was a steady stream of traffic heading down to Big Ben, but standing there on the steps Lucy felt as if the two of them were quite alone in the heart of the city.

'Th-thank you,' she stammered, only to catch her breath as Guy reached out and put his hands at her waist to draw her down the last step towards him.

'I'd really like to kiss you,' he said softly. 'I've been thinking about it all night, ever since you opened the door wearing that dress. No, longer than that. Since the last time I kissed you. Can I kiss you again?'

'I don't…don't think that…would be a very good idea,' Lucy managed with difficulty. She had forgotten how to talk properly. Her voice was staggering up and down the scales, and she kept taking a breath in the wrong places so that her words came out sounding most peculiar.

And all the time Guy's hands were sliding warmly around, pulling her into his body, making it even harder to think.

'Why not?' he murmured, kissing the side of her neck, and she shivered.

'Because…because…' Lucy's senses were reeling and her mind seemed to have given up on the effort required to string a few coherent words together.

His lips were drifting tantalisingly along her jaw. 'That's not a good enough reason,' he said, teasing laughter rippling through his voice.

'Why kiss me, then?' she asked unsteadily.

'Because…because…' His mouth was very close to hers now. 'Don't you want me to?' he whispered.

That was unfair. He must know that every fibre of her was screaming *Yes! Yes! Kiss me now! Kiss me for ever!* Lucy swallowed. 'It's not that, it's just…'

'That you don't want to admit that you *do* want me to?' Guy murmured against her mouth, and Lucy couldn't hold out any longer.

'Yes,' she said, and felt his lips curve in a smile the moment before they possessed hers.

She melted into him, winding her arms around his neck and parting her lips so that she could kiss him back the way she had longed to do. It was bliss to be able to taste him, to tangle her fingers in his hair, to press against all that lovely, lean, muscled strength while her body sang and her senses spun and everything in her screamed out for more.

'Lucy,' said Guy breathlessly as he came up for air. 'Lucy…' He took her face between hands that were not quite steady, his eyes dark and urgent. 'Come back to the flat with me.'

Lucy was trembling. 'No,' she said and that tiny word was one of the hardest things that she had ever had to say. 'No, that really *wouldn't* be a good idea.'

'Are you going to pretend that you don't want to again?' he asked, frustration edging his voice.

'No,' she said shakily. 'There's not much point in denying that I want to, but I'm not going to. We're working together, Guy. I'm leaving soon. What's the point in getting involved?'

'We could have a good time together.'

No, because I want to marry you and spend the rest of my life with you.

But of course Guy wasn't going to say that. She wasn't the kind of girl he would marry. She was a fun girl, a girl to have a good time with. A temporary kind of girl who had temporary jobs and temporary boyfriends and moved on.

Now temporary wasn't enough—now she wanted forever.

Furious with herself for having hoped for even a nanosecond that he would say that he loved her, Lucy pulled away.

'You were the one who told me I should grow up, Guy. You said I could be more than a party girl. You told me I could change,' she said. 'Well, I have, so don't complain now because you'd actually rather I still just cared about having fun. It's too late for that now.'

CHAPTER TEN

LUCY took a deep breath and knocked on the door of Guy's office.

'Come in.'

He was sitting behind his desk when she went in, looking distant and abstracted, but the blue eyes sharpened at the sight of her.

'Lucy,' he said. 'To what do I owe the pleasure?'

She hadn't been alone with him since he had taken her home from Trafalgar Square, and the kiss had never been mentioned again. Lucy had tortured herself all weekend, imagining how things would have been if she had gone home with Guy as he had wanted, but she knew that she had made the right decision. It would have been wonderful, and, yes, they might have had fun for a couple of weeks, but when the party was over, what then? She needed more than fun now.

'Sheila said that you could spare me a couple of minutes.' Her heart was lodged high and tight in her throat, making it hard to speak.

'Have you got a problem with the organisation of the party?'

'No…well, yes, in a way…'

'We'd better sit down, then.' Guy got up from behind his desk and gestured her to the sofas.

Lucy perched on the edge of one, her hands clutched together to stop herself reaching for him, and let her eyes rest on his hungrily. There was an uncharacteristically strained look around his mouth and he looked as if he were sleeping as badly as she was.

She had hardly seen him since the Sheldons' party. She had been genuinely busy, sending out cleverly worded invitations, cajoling caterers, confirming marquees, chasing up entertainers, rethinking decorations and intriguing the media, but the plans for the fund raising party had also been a good excuse to avoid Guy. On the few occasions they had met, they had been meticulously polite to each other and Lucy had hated it. Only desperation had brought her to him now.

'What is it?' asked Guy, settling opposite her.

Lucy drew a steadying breath. 'I'm going to have to go back to Australia,' she said baldly.

He went very still for a moment. 'Now?'

She nodded miserably. 'As soon as possible, yes.'

'Can't it wait? It's only a couple of weeks until the party. I need you here to make sure it all goes off the way you've planned. It's too late to get in yet another person,' he said, a spark of anger in his eyes. 'You can't walk out on me now, Lucy.'

'I don't want to,' she said wretchedly. 'But this is something I have to do for Meredith.'

'For Meredith?' Guy frowned. 'What's this about?'

'I went to see Richard yesterday,' she told him. 'They're letting him go home soon, and he was talking about Meredith. He does that quite a lot. Last night, he went on and on about what a good friend she was and how much he missed talking to her, and I think—I'm *sure*—that if she were here, he'd realise that she's the one he really loves.

'And Meredith loves him,' Lucy went on, desperate to

make Guy understand. 'She says she's over him, but I know that she isn't. If only she could come back, I know they would get together and she could be happy. Meredith deserves that more than anyone. She won't come back as long as I'm here, though, and I'm afraid that if she waits too long, Richard will get on with his life. That nurse, Mairi, is already sniffing around.'

The words were tumbling out of her now and Lucy made herself stop and draw a breath. 'I thought about this all last night. I've thought and I've thought…I know I'll be letting you down,' she said desperately, 'but I owe Meredith so much. If I go back to fulfil my contract with Hal, she'll be able to come home, and she'll have a chance to be happy. I have to do that for her, Guy,' she said in a low voice. 'I'm sorry, but I did promise Hal that I would go back before Meredith could leave.'

'I spoke to Hal the other day when he rang Ma to see how she was,' said Guy after a moment. 'He told me that Emma and Mickey had gone back to Sydney.'

'Yes, Meredith emailed me that, too. But Hal still needs a cook.'

Getting to his feet, Guy prowled over to the glass wall and stood looking out at St Paul's. 'What's this really about, Lucy?' he asked abruptly. 'Do you *want* to go back?'

'No,' she admitted.

'So it's not about Kevin?'

'No,' she said, startled that he even remembered Kevin. 'I realised a long time ago that I was just in love with the idea of him. He was a kind of fantasy figure, I suppose. It wasn't real.'

The tension in Guy's shoulders relaxed and he turned round. 'Then tell Hal how you feel,' he said. 'I know him. He's not going to want you back unless you really want to be there, and now that Emma and Mickey have gone he'll be able to manage without you. Ask him if he'll let Meredith come home. Tell him why.'

'What about my promise?' said Lucy uncertainly.

'You promised to make the party fun, too,' he reminded her with a faint smile. 'It won't be unless you're there.'

She bit her lip. 'I'm sure someone else could take over.'

'It's too late for that.' Guy shook his head. 'No, I need you here. I've put a lot of trust in you, Lucy. I know you've been working really hard and that you've got some great ideas. You can't just walk out now. There's also the issue of our so-called engagement…or have you forgotten that?'

'Perhaps it's time we called it off,' said Lucy. 'I'm sure people must have noticed that we haven't been spending time together.'

'They think we're making a big effort to keep our personal and professional lives separate. They probably all imagine that we're spending fabulously romantic evenings together. Only you and I know that's not true,' he said in a dry voice.

Lucy's eyes dropped first.

'Look, it's only another couple of weeks,' Guy said. 'Ring Hal and see what he says. If there's a problem, I'll talk to him, but I want you here to make sure that party is a success and that we can build that paediatric unit for Michael. It'll mean a lot to my mother if we can raise enough money to do it soon.'

'And the engagement?'

'Let's agree to have an argument there, after which I'll tell anyone who asks that it's all off. That was your suggestion, after all,' he said with a glimmer of his old smile. 'After that, you're free to go where you like, do what you want. But the party comes first. It's time for you to finish something, Lucy.'

Fireworks exploded above Lucy's head in a dazzling display of colour and noise, and she smiled at the *oohs* and *aahs* that rose around her. Even the most jaded sophisticate found it hard

to resist a firework display. There was something so...
celebratory about the whoosh and the bang and the burst of
sparkling light.

'So this is where you are.'

The sound of Guy's voice sent Lucy's pulse whooshing
upwards along with the fireworks and she turned to see him,
immaculate as ever in a dinner jacket and bow-tie. She had
been aware of him circulating amongst the guests, smiling,
welcoming, making everyone he spoke to feel an essential
part of the party, but she had deliberately avoided him.

She had worked so hard to make the party a success and
she was pleased, of course, that it had exceeded all her expectations, but with the fulfilment of that promise came the
dull realisation that this was the end. After tonight, she would
no longer have a job at Dangerfield & Dunn. That stupid pretence that she was engaged to Guy would be over and she
would have no further excuse to see him at all.

And now here he was, and she was going to have to find
a way to say goodbye.

'I've been looking all over for you,' said Guy.

'I've been behind the scenes mostly,' said Lucy.

'Well, whatever you've been doing, it's worked. You've
done a fantastic job. Everyone keeps telling me what a great
time they're having, and the Chief Executive of the hospital
can't wipe the smile off her face. I thought you'd be good,
but I didn't realise you'd be *this* good.'

Lucy swallowed. 'Thank you for giving me the opportunity to organise it.' Her voice sounded high and stiff. 'I've
learnt a lot about events management.'

Guy looked at her. She was wearing the little black dress
that she had worn to the Sheldons' party. It brought back bit-
tersweet memories, but she could hardly leave it sitting in the
wardrobe just because he had kissed her. It was Lucy's only

smart dress, and it was special. She had wanted to wear it to-night when she said goodbye.

Her throat tightened horribly at the thought, and above their heads the fireworks exploded in a spectacular finale, then fizzled out. Like her time with Guy, she thought pain-fully.

'You look beautiful,' said Guy suddenly. 'You shouldn't be hiding out here. Come and dance.'

'No, I…' Lucy couldn't bear to smile, to laugh, to pretend any more. She was going to have to say goodbye some time. Better to do it now, in the dark. 'It's so hot in those marquees,' she said. 'I'm enjoying the cool.'

'OK,' he said, his eyes never leaving her face. 'Shall we walk for a bit?'

She nodded. *Just say it*, she told herself sternly. Say, *It's time we said goodbye, Guy. It won't be so hard.* But she couldn't unlock her jaw to get the words out.

They walked around the gardens in silence for a while, Lucy desperately storing up memories of the way he moved, the way he turned his head, the tilt at the corner of his mouth.

'Hal told me you rang,' said Guy at last. 'He said Meredith had come home.'

'She did, yes, but that was another thing I got wrong,' said Lucy bitterly. 'It turns out that Richard isn't in love with either of us. He's more interested in that sneaky little nurse.'

She hugged her arms together, remembering her dismay when Meredith had told her what had happened at the hos-pital. 'I thought I could make Meredith's dream come true but it was all for nothing,' she said sadly. 'I shouldn't have said anything. I should have waited until I was sure, instead of rais-ing her hopes like that.' Lucy bit her lip. 'I keep thinking that I've learnt how to be responsible, but I keep getting things wrong.'

'You can't make your sister's dreams come true,' said Guy. 'She has to do that for herself. We all have to do that.'

Lucy mustered a smile. 'Well, I'm working on mine,' she told him.

'You are?' He stopped and looked at her. 'How?'

'I've decided that I'm going to make a career for myself in events management,' she told him brightly. 'I'm going to set up my own company.'

There was a tiny pause. 'Good for you,' said Guy.

'I've even picked up a client tonight, and several people have asked for my card.'

'That's great. No, I mean it,' he said, as if hearing the flatness in his voice. 'I think you'll do brilliantly.'

'So it looks as if it's time to move on.' Lucy was breathing very carefully. 'It's probably time we had that argument, in fact.'

'What argument?'

'The one that makes you realise that I'm the last woman you'd want to spend your life with, and makes me throw my non-existent ring back in your face.'

'Oh, that argument.' They had walked some way from the marquees, but the night air was alive with the sound of voices and laughter, a mocking counterpoint to the tension pooling around them. 'If that's what you want,' said Guy in a hard voice.

'Well…it's what we agreed,' she said, swallowing the lump in her throat.

His eyes looked into hers. 'What are we going to argue about?'

'I…I guess I could complain about the way you flirt with other women,' she tried to joke, but he didn't smile back.

'I don't.'

'Or you could say that I'm too frivolous and silly for you.'

'You're not.'

'Then perhaps we could just decide that we're incompatible.'

'Are we?'

Lucy made herself look away from his gaze. 'I think so, Guy,' she said painfully. 'It's not you, it's me,' she tried to explain. 'You know who you are. You know what you want to do. I feel as if I need to find myself, *do* something for myself.'

She paused. 'When I came to your office that time, you told me to finish organising this party. Finish something, you said, and I realised that I'd never done that before. This is the first project I've seen through to the end. I just drift along, never getting to grips with anything...I don't really know who I am or what I can do,' she told him. 'I need to find that out on my own.'

Her voice was starting to wobble and she took a deep breath. 'I want you to know, though, that the last few weeks have been some of the happiest I've ever had—and I've had lots of happy weeks. I've really enjoyed working for Dangerfield & Dunn, and I'm more grateful than I can say for the opportunities you've given me. And...and it's going to break my heart to say goodbye,' she finished in a rush.

'Then why say it?' asked Guy.

'Because I need to know if what I feel for you is real,' she said, meeting his eyes fully at last. 'Or is it just like what I felt for Kevin? I could tell you that I loved you, Guy; how could you ever believe me, even if you wanted to hear it? How can I be sure of it myself? I want to find a way to prove it to myself. Can you understand that?' she asked anxiously.

He sighed. 'In a way,' he said at last. 'I understand that you need some time to work things out for yourself, anyway. So...' He took her hands and found a smile. 'We'd better have that argument, then. You go first.'

Lucy's smile wavered but she pressed her lips together to stop it falling apart. 'Guy, you're a horrible person,' she said, her eyes on his.

'And you're no fun,' he replied. His clasp was warm and steadying and it was as if they were having two completely separate conversations. Their mouths said one thing, their eyes the opposite.

'Your jokes are terrible.'

'You're not that pretty, you know, Cinders,' said Guy, drawing her closer.

Lucy's throat was so tight by now that she could hardly speak. She didn't think she could go on much longer. 'I hate you,' she whispered against his cheek.

'I hate you, too,' said Guy, and turned his head so that their lips could meet in a long, tender kiss of farewell.

Lucy let herself hold him one last time. Her arms slid around his back and she clung to him while she kissed him in a way that she hoped told him better than words ever could how much she loved him.

Her heart cracked when at last she made herself step back and out of his arms. Guy resisted for a moment, as if he didn't want to let her go, but then his hands dropped and she was free.

'Thank you, Guy,' she said, her voice wobbling horribly. 'Thank you for everything.'

And then she turned and walked away from him, as fast as she could, before she could change her mind.

'Lucy!' Imogen looked up in delighted surprise. 'I wasn't expecting to see you! Does this mean you've come back?' she added hopefully.

'No.' Lucy felt terrible. She had only been back at Dangerfield & Dunn a matter of seconds and already three people had told her how pleased they were to see her back. 'I've just come in to collect my stuff.'

'Oh.' Imogen's face fell. 'I was hoping you'd have changed your mind. It's not the same here without you.'

'I was only here for about a month!'

'It felt like longer. We all miss you, and I'm sure Guy misses you, too,' Imogen went on. 'He hasn't been the same since. I mean, he's still lovely and he's always friendly, but it's like now he's trying, and before he didn't have to.' She shook her head. 'I couldn't believe it when I heard you two had split up. You seemed so perfect for each other. What happened?'

'We just agreed that it wasn't going to work out,' said Lucy after a moment.

'That's what Guy said.' Imogen sounded dissatisfied. 'No one can understand it, though. You were so obviously meant for each other!'

Lucy smiled painfully. 'We weren't really, Imogen. We might have looked OK together, but we're very different people. I'm not the right girl for Guy.'

She had been reminding herself of that continually over the past three weeks. Guy was a serious person, and he needed a serious wife. Not someone who didn't know how to laugh, but someone responsible, someone intelligent and steady who knew herself and knew Guy. A grown-up.

She had never really grown up, Lucy realised. She had just played at life, and she had been lucky because she had been able to get by doing that. But falling in love with Guy had taught her that sometimes having a good time wasn't enough. She could have spent the past three weeks with him. They could have made love every night and laughed during the day, and it would have been wonderful, but it wouldn't have lasted.

And loving Guy, really loving him, her heart would have broken when it was over.

Lucy had made her decision. If she wanted to spend her life with him, the way she so desperately did, she was going to have to prove that she was more than just a temporary girl. She was going to set up her own business and make it a success and accomplish something on her own. And then, only then, would she go back to Guy.

He might not like the new Lucy. He might prefer fun and frivolity. He might not be interested in forever, whatever she had done. But Lucy was prepared for all of that. Deep in the core of her, she knew that whatever happened with Guy, this was something that she had to do for herself.

It didn't mean that it was easy. Missing Guy was a dull, constant ache in the pit of her stomach. She had done her best to keep busy, throwing herself into her new job and finding out about how to set up her own business as an events manager, but she hadn't realised what a gaping void he would leave in her life.

'I don't understand what the problem is,' Meg had said, exasperated, dragging Lucy away from the computer where she had been researching websites until her eyes were out on stalks, because anything was better than letting herself think about Guy.

'You're miserable,' Meg told her sternly as she handed her a glass of wine. 'You want him. It sounds as if he wants you. He's straight, single, good-looking and obscenely rich and, let me tell you, guys like that do *not* grow on trees! There are millions of women out there who would snap him up in a moment, including me, and if you mess around like this he'll be up for grabs.' Meg shook her head. 'If you lose him, Lucy, you'll only have yourself to blame. Just ring him!'

'I *can't*,' Lucy said, holding the glass to her chest with both hands as if for comfort. 'It would be like admitting that I wasn't serious when I said I wanted to prove myself. He'll think that I've given up already, just like I've always done before.'

'You don't have to give up the business. You just want to see him—or are you going to try and pretend that you don't?'

'No. I want to see him so much it hurts, but I'm afraid that, if I do, I'll lose my focus,' she said. 'I'll just want to be with him, and I'll slide into my old ways and let him look after me, and it'll be lovely for a bit, and then Guy will get bored.'

'Why should he?'

'Because I'm not…oh, I don't know how to explain it…it's as if I'm not properly formed,' said Lucy. 'I'm all froth and fun. Guy deserves someone more than that, and maybe I can offer more than that; how will I ever know if I don't try and find it? And I think Guy understands that. At least, he didn't try and talk me out of it, and he hasn't rung,' she said. 'If he really cared, he could have rung me.'

'Maybe he's just confused by what you want—like me,' said Meg, but Lucy had stuck firm for once.

Part of her was hoping that her feelings for Guy would go the way of her other loves, and that if she didn't see him for a while she would start to forget him, but it hadn't worked like that. The longer they were apart, the more she missed him.

Lucy knew Meg thought she was mad. She knew quite well that men like Guy—tall, handsome and rich—were a fantasy for an awful lot of women, but it wasn't the fantasy she wanted. It was the real Guy. The Guy who let his mother grumble at him while he quietly got on with making her life easier. The Guy who had been a surfer. The Guy who made people laugh.

Guy, whose kiss turned her bones to honey and whose smile made her heart turn over.

That was the Guy she missed. She missed the warmth of his presence and the laugh in his voice and the way the world felt brighter and better and clearer when he was there.

'I'd better go,' she said awkwardly to Imogen as she glanced at her watch. 'I told Sheila I'd be there by now.'

In fact, she had made a point of checking with Sheila that Guy would be out when she came to collect the things she had left in her office before the party. She didn't want to run the risk of meeting him and seeing all her fine resolutions crumble to dust.

It didn't take long to empty her desk, although it was still surprising how much stuff she had managed to accumulate in a month. Sheila gave her a box and into it went a pair of gloves she'd thought she'd lost, assorted cosmetics, photographs, a couple of books she had never got round to reading, her camera—what was *that* doing there?—a half-eaten packet of biscuits, a box of tissues, some change and a pot plant that Imogen had given her to celebrate having an office to herself for the first time ever.

Lucy allowed herself one last nostalgic look round, and then she went to say goodbye to Sheila.

Carrying her box, she pressed the button for the lift and stared ferociously ahead, trying not to cry. 'Come on, come on,' she muttered, desperate in case anyone came along to share the lift.

At last it arrived and, to her relief, it didn't stop until the ground floor. Lucy hoisted her box up into her arms, waited for the lift to settle and took a step forward as the doors slid open.

And there stood Guy.

Lucy's whole body seemed to leap with joy at the sight of him, but she stood stock still, as if rooted to the floor of the lift, torn between shock and relief, elation and dismay.

'Lucy!' Guy seemed equally stunned by coming face to face with her so unexpectedly and a couple of other people waiting to get in looked from him to Lucy and then to each other, and then by tacit consent moved tactfully aside to wait for one of the other lifts.

Guy swallowed. 'I wasn't expecting to see you,' he said at last, eyes blue and hungry as they devoured her face.

'Sheila said you'd be out,' Lucy managed, clutching her

box to her chest. At least it was something to hold on to while her heart was hammering like a mad thing and her knees felt so weak that she was afraid she might crumple to the floor at any minute.

'I was supposed to be at a meeting, but when I got there—'

The doors chose that moment to assume that anyone who wanted to get in would have done so and began to close. Guy leapt forward to stop them, holding them back with a hand.

'It was cancelled. Some family crisis,' he said, without taking his eyes from her face. 'Why am I telling you this, anyway? I'm babbling like an idiot just because you're here…!'

'I came to get my things,' said Lucy unsteadily. It was just like the last time, when two completely separate conversations were going on at the same time. She couldn't tear her eyes from his. It was just so good to see him, to hear him, to be near him again.

No, no, this isn't right! Her mind struggled desperately to regain control of the situation. *You can't give in yet. Remember all that stuff about proving yourself? Well, do it. Say goodbye and go.*

'Did Sheila know you were coming? She didn't tell me.'

'I asked her not to,' she said. 'I thought it would be easier if I didn't see you.'

'Why?'

Lucy just shook her head and Guy stepped into the lift. 'Why, Lucy?' he persisted.

Get on with it! Lucy's mind ordered, and she made to step past him with the box in her arms. 'I should go,' she said feebly, but he was blocking the way.

'I don't want you to go. I miss you too much.'

Behind him, more people were heading to the lifts and veering away at the last minute as they realised that a scene was in progress. 'I've got a new job,' said Lucy, her voice wobbling ridiculously. 'I'm committed to that now.'

'I'm not talking about work,' said Guy, sounding almost angry. 'I miss *you.* I can't concentrate on anything. I don't want to eat, I can't sleep. Look at me, I'm a mess!'

'Guy, this just makes things harder…'

'What does? Seeing you? Talking to you? It doesn't feel harder to me. Sitting at home, missing you, that's what feels hard.'

'It is for me,' she said, stung into a response at last. 'I knew it would be like this!' she said wildly. 'I knew I'd see you and I'd just want to give up everything just to be able to touch you, but I can't do that.'

A smile hovered around Guy's mouth suddenly. 'Why don't we touch and then talk about what you have to give up?' he said, taking the box from her and putting it on the floor.

'Don't joke about this!' Lucy turned her head away, biting her lip. 'I'm serious. I'm trying to change my life here, and you're not helping.'

'Lucy,' said Guy as the doors closed behind him, cutting them off from the interested crowd. 'What is it you want to change?'

'Me,' she said. 'I've always been a temporary person. I have temporary jobs and temporary relationships, but I don't want that any more. I want a real job and a real relationship. You were the one who told me that I always had to be rescued, Guy, and you were right. I've spent my whole life relying on other people one way or another. Well, now I want to do something for myself. I want to set up my own business, and make a success of it.'

'Why would touching me change that?'

'Because I would get distracted. I love you, and I know you won't believe me,' said Lucy almost crossly, 'but I do.'

A smile started at the back of his eyes. 'Usually if you love someone, touching is good,' he said as he took her hands, but she pulled them away.

'How long for, though?'

'How about for ever?'

Lucy stared at him. The lift doors, tired of waiting to be told which floor to go to, sighed open once more, but neither Lucy nor Guy noticed the interested looks of the small crowd that had gathered.

'You can't want me for ever,' she said unsteadily.

'Can't I?' Guy pretended to consider the matter. 'Do you know, I think I can. I think I do.'

'But…' She swallowed. 'I'm not a serious enough person for you.'

'Lucy, you *are* a serious person,' he said, repossessing her hands. 'You're warm and funny and loyal and brave, and you have a gift for happiness and enjoying life that is worth more than any qualification, any career, any profit margin on a business! You don't pretend to be anything you're not—unless it's my fiancée, of course!—and people like you because of that. Who was it everyone turned to in a crisis when you were on reception here? Who got on and sorted things out for Sheila when her father was ill? Who gave up a job she loved for a sister she loved more?'

With a sigh, the doors closed again.

'But those things aren't…'

'Aren't what? Aren't important? They are, Lucy. You don't need to prove yourself. You just need to *be* yourself.'

His hands were warm and sustaining around hers. Longing to believe him, Lucy's fingers curled around his in spite of herself.

'I wanted to prove that I really did love you,' she confessed. 'It's hardly any time since I told you I was in love with Kevin, and this feels so, so different…but I can't see how you could believe me that it was true.'

'You don't need to prove anything to me, Cinders,' said Guy. 'How can you prove that you love someone? Love isn't a deal. You can't say, I'll love you if you're like this or you do this, and you can't test for it. All we can do is love each other and believe in each other, and maybe when we cut our golden anniversary cake we can say look, there's the proof, but we can't do that now. We just have to trust each other, and trust in how we feel.'

Lucy couldn't see very clearly. Her eyes were blurred with the tears that trembled on the ends of her lashes.

'All I'm trying to say, Lucy, is that I love you as you are,' said Guy. 'I know you can do whatever you want to do, and I know you want to prove that to yourself. When you told me that at the party, I thought you wanted me to stand back and let you do it by yourself, I thought that was what you needed, so that's what I've been trying to do. I told myself then that I would give you a month, and then I would tell you what *I* needed.'

'Which is?' whispered Lucy.

'Which is just to be with you,' he said. 'You can do it by yourself, Lucy. I just want to be by your side when you do. I don't want to help you or do it for you, I just want to cheer you on, and when you have setbacks, as you will, I want to be there to hold you and tell you that I believe in you, that you are the best events manager there has ever been.'

Resigned, the doors opened again.

'Guy…' Lucy had lost her battle with the tears. She reached blindly for him and Guy kicked the box aside and yanked her into his arms and kissed her, and as she sank into him, giddy with relief and happiness, there was a burst of applause from those waiting who had been watching the story in the lift unfold with naked interest.

'About time!' someone shouted, and Guy grinned as he reached out and pressed the button for the penthouse floor.

They kissed all the way up to the top floor, and all the way back down again because they didn't notice that the lift had stopped. They were interrupted once on their way back up when the doors opened and an embarrassed voice said, 'Oh, excuse me,' but then they were on their way back to the ground floor. A beaming Imogen sent them back up to the penthouse floor again, where Sheila was waiting to haul them out of the lift.

'Imogen says you're causing a traffic jam down there,' she said calmly. 'You've got a perfectly good office to do that kind of thing in, so why don't you go in and let the rest of us use the lifts?'

Shaking her head, she retrieved the box as Guy led Lucy, reeling with happiness, into his office and firmly closed the door.

'I'm so happy,' she said, blizzarding kisses over his face as they tumbled on to one of the sofas. 'I love you so much, I can't believe you love me!'

'I think I've loved you ever since I walked into the kitchen at Wirrindago and found you looking down your nose at me,' said Guy.

'I thought you were awful,' Lucy admitted. 'I couldn't wait for you to leave…and look at me now!'

He hesitated. 'No regrets about going back to Australia, then?'

'No,' said Lucy. 'But I think I might be going back some time soon. It turns out that Meredith is in love with Hal, and she's sold her house so that she can go back to Wirrindago to be with him.'

'Hal and Meredith…?' A slow smile spread over Guy's face as he considered it as a new possibility. 'Do you think that'll work?'

'Do you think *we'll* work?' she countered.

'Yes,' he said immediately, smoothing her hair lovingly away from her face. 'It will if we're prepared to work at it, to love each other and remember to have fun. And it would be hard not to have fun with you, Lucy. I only have to look at you and I want to smile.'

'That doesn't sound as if you take me very seriously,' said Lucy, only half-joking.

'But I do,' he said, and his gaze was very steady. 'It's true that I resisted you at first. I did my best to pretend that I wasn't smitten. I told myself that I didn't need a scatty blonde, but the more I got to know you, the more I realised that there's so much more to you than your capacity to have a good time.' He smiled at her, very tenderly. 'Even at the rodeo, when you wanted to stay at the party, you came back with me because you're a girl who keeps her promises.'

'I am.' Lucy rolled on top of him, pressing her lips to his throat. 'I'll promise you anything you want!'

'Really?' He brightened. 'In that case, will you tell my mother to stop hassling me about getting you back?'

She laughed down at him. 'I will.'

'And will you promise to love me for ever?'

'Oh, yes.' Lucy sighed. 'I will, I will.'

Guy's eyes were very blue as he gazed up at her. 'Will you marry me, Cinders?'

Lucy held his face between her hands and looked lovingly down into his eyes. 'I promise,' she said, and kissed him.

* * * * *

Brad shoved the truck into gear and drove to the bottom of the hill, where the road forked. Turn left, and he'd be home in five minutes. Turn right, and he was headed for Indian Rock.

He had no damn business going to Indian Rock.

He had nothing to say to Meg McKettrick, and if he never set eyes on the woman again, it would be two weeks too soon.

He turned right.

He couldn't have said why.

He just drove straight to the Dixie Dog Drive-In.

Back in the day, he and Meg used to meet at the Dixie Dog, by tacit agreement, when either of them had been away. It had been some kind of universe thing, purely intuitive.

Passing familiar landmarks, Brad told himself he ought to turn around. The old days were gone. Things had ended badly between him and Meg anyhow, and she wasn't going to be at the Dixie Dog.

He kept driving.

He rounded a bend, and there was the Dixie Dog. Its big neon sign, a giant hot dog, was all lit up and going through its corny sequence—first it was covered in red squiggles of light, meant to suggest ketchup, and then yellow, for mustard.

Brad pulled into one of the slots next to a speaker, rolled down the truck window and ordered.

A girl roller-skated out with the order about five minutes later.

When she wheeled up to the driver's window, smiling, her eyes went wide with recognition, and she dropped the tray with a clatter.

Silently Brad swore. Damn if he hadn't forgotten he was a famous country singer.

The girl, a skinny thing wearing too much eye makeup, immediately started to cry. "I'm sorry!" she sobbed, squatting to gather up the mess.

"It's okay," Brad answered quietly, leaning to look down at her, catching a glimpse of her plastic name tag. "It's okay, Mandy. No harm done."

"I'll get you another dog and a shake right away, Mr. O'Ballivan!"

"Mandy?"

She stared up at him pitifully, sniffling. Thanks to the copious tears, most of the goop on her eyes had slid south. "Yes?"

"When you go back inside, could you not mention seeing me?"

"But you're Brad O'Ballivan!"

"Yeah," he answered, suppressing a sigh. "I know."

She rolled a little closer. "You wouldn't happen to have a picture you could autograph for me, would you?"

"Not with me," Brad answered.

"You could sign this napkin, though," Mandy said. "It's only got a little chocolate on the corner."

Brad took the paper napkin and her order pen, and scrawled his name. Handed both items back through the window.

She turned and whizzed back toward the side entrance to the Dixie Dog.

Brad waited, marveling that he hadn't considered incidents like this one before he'd decided to come back home. In retrospect, it seemed shortsighted, to say the least, but the truth was, he'd expected to be—Brad O'Ballivan.

Presently Mandy skated back out again, and this time she managed to hold on to the tray.

"I didn't tell a soul!" she whispered. "But Heather and Darlene *both* asked me why my mascara was all smeared." Efficiently she hooked the tray onto the bottom edge of the window.

Brad extended payment, but Mandy shook her head.

"The boss said it's on the house, since I dumped your first order on the ground."

He smiled. "Okay, then. Thanks."

Mandy retreated, and Brad was just reaching for the food when a bright red Blazer whipped into the space beside his. The driver's door sprang open, crashing into the metal speaker, and somebody got out in a hurry.

Something quickened inside Brad.

And in the next moment Meg McKettrick was standing practically on his running board, her blue eyes blazing.

Brad grinned. "I guess you're not over me after all," he said.

Silhouette®

SPECIAL EDITION™

**brings you a heartwarming
new McKettrick's story from**

NEW YORK TIMES BESTSELLING AUTHOR

LINDA LAEL MILLER

THE
McKETTRICK
Way

Meg McKettrick is surprised to be reunited
with her high school flame, Brad O'Ballivan,
who has returned home to his family's
neighboring ranch. After seeing Meg again,
Brad realizes he still loves her. But the pride
of both manage to interfere with love...until
an unexpected matchmaker gets involved.

—— McKettrick Women ——

Available December wherever you buy books.

Visit Silhouette Books at www.eHarlequin.com SSEIBC24867

ATHENA FORCE

*Heart-pounding romance
and thrilling adventure.*

She's their ace in the hole.

Posing as a glamorous high roller, Bethany James, a
professional gambler and sometimes government agent,
uncovers a mob boss's deadly secrets…and the ugly sins
from his past. But when a daredevil with a tantalizing
drawl calls her bluff, the stakes—and her heart rate—
become much, much higher. Beth can't help but wonder:
Have the cards been finally stacked against her?

ATHENA FORCE

Will the women of Athena unravel Arachne's
powerful web of blackmail and death…or succumb
to their enemies' deadly secrets?

Look for

STACKED DECK
by *Terry Watkins*.

Available December wherever you buy books.

REQUEST YOUR FREE BOOKS!
2 FREE NOVELS PLUS 2
FREE GIFTS!

HARLEQUIN ROMANCE®

From the Heart, For the Heart

YES! Please send me 2 FREE Harlequin Romance® novels and my 2 FREE gifts. After receiving them, if I don't wish to receive any more books, I can return the shipping statement marked "cancel." If I don't cancel, I will receive 4 brand-new novels every month and be billed just $3.57 per book in the U.S., or $4.05 per book in Canada, plus 25¢ shipping and handling per book and applicable taxes, if any*. That's a savings of over 15% off the cover price! I understand that accepting the 2 free books and gifts places me under no obligation to buy anything. I can always return a shipment and cancel at any time. Even if I never buy another book from Harlequin, the two free books and gifts are mine to keep forever.

114 HDN EEV7 314 HDN EEWK

Name _____ (PLEASE PRINT) _____

Address _____ Apt. _____

City _____ State/Prov. _____ Zip/Postal Code _____

Signature (if under 18, a parent or guardian must sign)

Mail to the **Harlequin Reader Service®**:
IN U.S.A.: P.O. Box 1867, Buffalo, NY 14240-1867
IN CANADA: P.O. Box 609, Fort Erie, Ontario L2A 5X3

Not valid to current Harlequin Romance subscribers.

Want to try two free books from another line?
Call 1-800-873-8635 or visit www.morefreebooks.com.

* Terms and prices subject to change without notice. NY residents add applicable sales tax. Canadian residents will be charged applicable provincial taxes and GST. This offer is limited to one order per household. All orders subject to approval. Credit or debit balances in a customer's account(s) may be offset by any other outstanding balance owed by or to the customer. Please allow 4 to 6 weeks for delivery.

Your Privacy: Harlequin is committed to protecting your privacy. Our Privacy Policy is available online at www.eHarlequin.com or upon request from the Reader Service. From time to time we make our lists of customers available to reputable firms who may have a product or service of interest to you. If you would prefer we not share your name and address, please check here. ☐

HR07

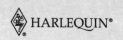

HARLEQUIN®

American ★ Romance®

Kate Merrill had grown up convinced
that the most attractive men were incapable
of ever settling down. Yet the harder she
resisted the superstar photographer
Tyler Nichols, the more persistent the
handsome world traveler became.
So by the time Christmas arrived, there
was only one wish on her holiday list—
that she was wrong!

LOOK FOR

THE CHRISTMAS DATE

BY

Michele Dunaway

**Available December
wherever you buy books**

www.eHarlequin.com

HAR75195

Get ready to meet

THREE WISE WOMEN

with stories by

DONNA BIRDSELL, LISA CHILDS

and

SUSAN CROSBY.

Don't miss these three unforgettable stories about modern-day women and the love and new lives they find on Christmas.

Look for *Three Wise Women*
Available December wherever you buy books.

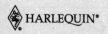

HARLEQUIN *Romance*

Coming Next Month

**In a month filled with Christmas sparkle, we bring you tycoons
and bosses, loves lost and found, little miracles that change your life
and always, always a happy ending!**

#3991 SNOWBOUND WITH MR. RIGHT Judy Christenberry
Mistletoe & Marriage
Sally loves Christmastime in the small town of Bailey, with the snow
softly falling and all the twinkling lights on the trees. But when handsome
stranger and city slicker Hunter arrives, everything seems different, and
she is in danger of losing her heart.

#3992 THE MILLIONAIRE TYCOON'S ENGLISH ROSE Lucy Gordon
The Rinucci Brothers
Ever heard the expression, to love someone is to set them free? Freedom
is precious to Celia, since she can't see. But she can live life to the full!
The last of the Rinucci brothers, Francesco, wants to wrap her in cotton
wool, but hadn't bargained on feisty Celia....

#3993 THE BOSS'S LITTLE MIRACLE Barbara McMahon
Career girl Anna doesn't have time for love. She's poised for promotion,
when in walks her new CEO, Tanner...the man who broke her heart a few
weeks ago! Then Anna discovers a little miracle has happened—and it
changes everything.

#3994 THEIR GREEK ISLAND REUNION Carol Grace
Even the most perfect relationships have cracks—as Olivia and Jack have
realized. Their marriage seems over, but Jack refuses to let go. He whisks
Olivia away to an idyllic Greek island. But will it be enough to give them a
forever-future together?

#3995 WIN, LOSE...OR WED! Melissa McClone
Love it or loathe it, reality TV is here to stay! Millie loathes it, after
irresistible bachelor Jace dumped her in front of millions of viewers. But in
aid of charity, she finds herself on a new show with Jace, and *everything* is
captured on camera—even their stolen kisses!

#3996 HIS CHRISTMAS ANGEL Michelle Douglas
Do you remember *that* guy? The one from your past that you loved
more than life itself, the one you never seem to be able to get over?
Imagine he's back in town, and more gorgeous than ever. Join Cassie
as boy-next-door Sol comes home for Christmas....